Books of Merit

MORE *in* ANGER

ALSO BY J. JILL ROBINSON

Saltwater Trees

Lovely in Her Bones

Eggplant Wife

Residual Desire

MORE *in* ANGER

a novel

J. JILL ROBINSON

THOMAS ALLEN PUBLISHERS
TORONTO

Copyright © 2012 J. Jill Robinson

All rights reserved. No part of this work may be reproduced or transmitted in any form or by any means—graphic, electronic, or mechanical, including photocopying, recording, taping, or information storage and retrieval systems—without the prior written permission of the publisher, or in the case of photocopying or other reprographic copying, a licence from the Canadian Copyright Licensing Agency.

Library and Archives Canada Cataloguing in Publication

Robinson, J. Jill, 1955-
More in anger : a novel / J. Jill Robinson.

ISBN 978-0-88762-953-2

I. Title.

PS8585.035166M67 2012 C813'.54 C2011-907121-5

Editor: Janice Zawerbny
Cover design: Michel Vrána
Cover images:
Wasp: Ale-ks / istockphoto.com
Wallpaper: tommaso lizzul / shutterstock.com
Text design: Gordon Robertson

Published by Thomas Allen Publishers,
a division of Thomas Allen & Son Limited,
390 Steelcase Road East,
Markham, Ontario L3R 1G2 Canada

www.thomasallen.ca

Canada Council for the Arts

The publisher gratefully acknowledges the support of The Ontario Arts Council for its publishing program.

We acknowledge the support of the Canada Council for the Arts, which last year invested $20.1 million in writing and publishing throughout Canada.

We acknowledge the Government of Ontario through the Ontario Media Development Corporation's Ontario Book Initiative.

We acknowledge the financial support of the Government of Canada through the Canada Book Fund for our publishing activities.

The author gratefully acknowledges the financial assistance of the Saskatchewan Arts Board and the Alberta Foundation for the Arts.

12 13 14 15 16 6 5 4 3 2

Text printed on a 100% PCW recycled stock

Printed and bound in Canada

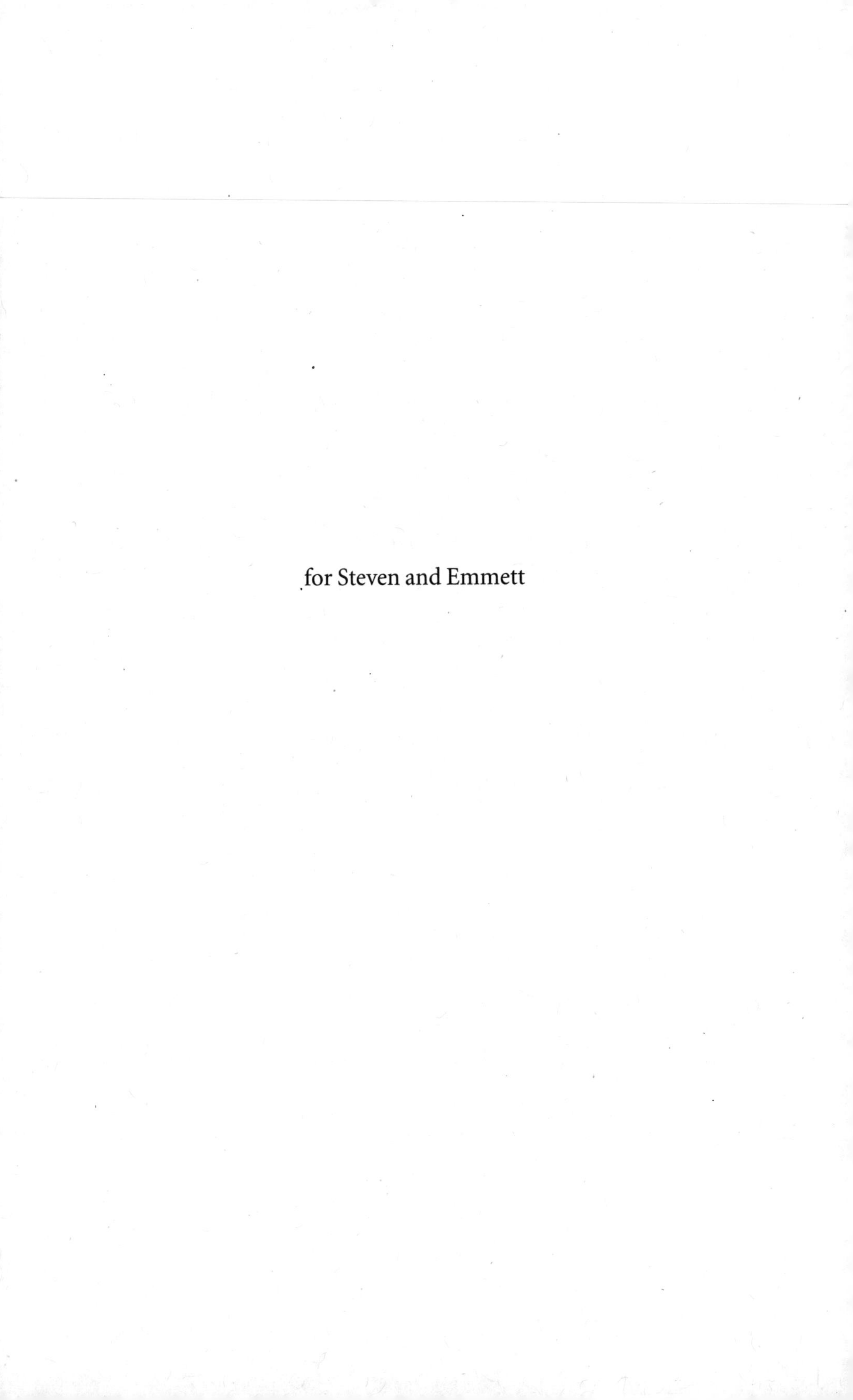

for Steven and Emmett

HAMLET: What, look'd he frowningly?

HORATIO: A countenance more in sorrow than in anger.

HAMLET (1.2.231)

MORE *in* ANGER

OPAL

The diamond in Opal's engagement ring glinted and sparkled as she sewed the skirt of her satin wedding dress, as she stitched the tiny seed pearls and faux orange blossoms onto her wedding veil. Every once in a while one of the ring's claws caught on the veil's netting, and Opal carefully released it. Engagement rings had become the latest fashion in 1913, and though she was not prone to pride, Opal had loved the ring the moment Mac presented it to her. Unaccustomed to wearing rings, she had been aware of the diamond's presence on her hand ever since he slid it onto her finger, its inherent coldness and hardness, and how it didn't give way when it pressed against her skin, or cloth, and everything that wasn't harder than itself. The diamond, just shy of a carat, was set on a very plain and narrow gold band etched finely and subtly with lines. The claws that tightly clutched the diamond were white gold, the round stone remarkable, Mac said, for its clarity and quality; it was, she thought, as clear as invisible must be. She looked at it often, held it up to the light.

Her *fiancé*—she loved the word—had now been gone from Winnipeg just over three years. Fortunately, she had discovered some pleasure in missing him; she found she enjoyed the yearning. She liked to sit alone, longing for his return, and imagine how their time together might *be* in the married years that lay just ahead. Coming closer every day.

Part of Mac's ongoing intrigue for her, she told herself, was wondering what lay beneath that hard, seemingly cold surface. She suspected a hot spring of affection and regard would be revealed once they were secured to each other by God, and after they became more accustomed to one another, more at home. She touched her cheek. Then, surreptitiously, her breast. He has chosen *me*, she thought happily. *Me*, instead of all the other girls in Winnipeg. In Scotland. In Canada. *Me!* "On June 9, 1915," she announced to herself in a whisper, her needle paused in the air, "Miss Opal Elizabeth King will be officially married to James 'Mac' Macaulay, solicitor for the Canadian Pacific Railway in Calgary." How happy she was. Finally, at twenty-five, she was going to be a wife.

Opal had met Mac Macaulay on May 10, 1909, when he walked through the door of the law firm where she worked. She remembered the day clearly, because it was the day she began wrestling with the new typing machine and she had black ink all over her hands and on one of her best white blouses. What a devilish contraption! The machine was supposed to make everyone's life so much easier, but the instruction book made no sense and the salesman was long gone.

It was snowing, but the last few days had been warm enough to soften the ground, so there was mud everywhere, thick gumbo mud that stuck like clay to the bottoms of boots, leaving tracks she would have to clean up again and again. Standing there with snow on the shoulders of his greatcoat, Mac spoke with a Scottish brogue so strong it took several repetitions before she understood that he wanted to meet with one of the partners, and she introduced him to Mr. Tupper. Mr. Macaulay was a serious-looking fellow, not tall, slight, with a straight, sharp nose and brown hair combed to one side. He nodded politely to her and attempted a small smile.

It was a totally different man who came out of Mr. Tupper's office an hour later. In spite of his obvious distress, he did remember to close the front door as he left, allowing her one final glimpse of his face, which was wet with tears and so black with emotion that it shook her badly. Several months later she dared to ask him what had happened. Mac had quickly learned from Mr. Tupper that it was English, not Scottish, law that was used in Canada, so in order to be called to the bar he would have to repeat his articles. This was particularly bad news for him, he told her, because he had just completed three years of articling in Edinburgh—twelve arduous hours of labour required daily, paid the equivalent of a dollar every two weeks, and wretched living conditions, which were all he could afford. He would tell her that he had made a vow to himself when he finished those hellish years that he would never again suffer like that—and now look what had happened. But thankfully, Mr. Tupper had offered him a job, and the conditions of his articling here were much better. Within weeks, Opal observed that the desperation in Mac's eyes had subsided, fading into a kind of grim determination, where it stayed.

At first Opal was shy around him—he seemed to take everything so seriously—but slowly she grew to like how he spoke, and how after several months had passed he relaxed enough that he sometimes teased her in a gruff, somewhat peculiar way that unfortunately was not always kind. But she forgave him: maybe that was how one joked in Scotland. His displays of humour were rare enough in any case; normally he remained extremely reserved, but impatient as he made his requests of her at work. And he remained difficult to know, though to all appearances he held the same high moral ideals as she.

Opal convinced herself early on that she and Mac were a good match, and she secretly liked to believe that God had directed him to her—all the way from Thornhill, Scotland, to Winnipeg, Manitoba, and then to that particular law firm on that particular day—and that His plan for them both was simply unfolding as it should. All she had to do was to be patient and have faith. Every night in her prayers she thanked Him, and every morning in her prayers she thanked Him again.

After a year or so Mac began to attend her church—Zion Methodist—and to walk with her from time to time for short distances if their paths should cross. She was not surprised, and she was pleased; His plan for them was unfolding. Eventually her patience paid off. Yes, she said to Mac after two full years had passed since that day in May. She would be glad to call him Mac instead of Mr. Macaulay when they were away from the office.

Opal was invited to the ceremony when Mac was called to the bar. She was so proud of him, and by then so deeply in love. But her heart was aching, too: he would be leaving Winnipeg. The Canadian Pacific Railway had invited him to work for them in Calgary. Because of the land boom in western Canada, speculation in the province had soared, and the CPR was of course heavily involved. In January 1912 the CPR had created the Department of Natural Resources and opened its Alberta offices, and they indicated that they wanted Mac, and they wanted him as soon as possible. He would start work for them on his thirtieth birthday, April 15, 1912. But what about her? she wanted to ask him but hadn't dared. He hadn't said a word about her. About her and him. Though they had become closer. He had held her hands. He had given her looks that suggested more than mere casual affection. He had come over for dinner many, many times, and enjoyed the company of her family. As he left their house, he always seemed warmer himself, and happier. What was to happen now? It was up to him.

At the farewell dinner the firm held for him, Mr. Tupper praised Mac, saying, "Macaulay is on his way to being a top-notch lawyer." And Mac's career prospects certainly pleased Opal's parents. Her father had observed approvingly, "Without question, that fellow is going places. No lack of inner fortitude. Sharp, shrewd, and suspicious. Attributes you need in the law. Note that," he added to his eldest son, Reg, who had just entered law school himself. Opal's mother, Georgie, head bent over the cross-stitched fireplace screen she was working on, nodded in agreement. "No one will ever put one over on *that* man." Opal's younger sisters, Lillie and Pearly K, just grinned from ear to ear as they always did whenever Mac's name came up.

Opal had hoped, even expected, that Mac would propose marriage to her before he left, but her prayers went unanswered. In fact, he didn't even kiss her goodbye, so caught up she supposed he was in the adventure that lay ahead for him, and overseeing his luggage's delivery to the baggage car, as well as his trunk full of books. Mac was distracted; he was excited about his new job, Opal said, sobbing against her mother's breast all the way home from the station.

But he hadn't abandoned her completely. He wrote to her, or to her and her family, once every two weeks, while Opal restricted herself to writing to him every Sunday night. In his first letter he mentioned how he had indeed celebrated his birthday by starting work, and that it would remain forever in his memory because it was also the day the *Titanic* went down—the news of the sinking was on Mr. Walker's desk when Mac went in that first day.

Opal took great care with her letters: Mac had made it clear that to him, language served a purpose, both in and out of business, and words beyond the conveyance of useful information reflected a "frivolity and excess" he found generally repugnant. In his opinion there was no point to much of anything or anyone that was not useful, which made it difficult for Opal to relax enough to write with confidence or pleasure. It wasn't only the *how* to write to him she found hard, but also the *what.* As a result she became terribly anxious each time she sat down, and sometimes went through half an inch of paper just trying to begin.

A year and a half later, Mac had returned to Winnipeg for a visit, and finally—finally!—he proposed marriage. They were standing together on the bank of the Assiniboine River, where they had been sharing a picnic that had taken her days to plan and prepare. Mac took both her hands in his and told her in an unlawyerish voice that shook with nervousness that he cared deeply for her and hoped they could forge a life together. And then he had knelt, getting grass stains on the knees of his trousers, and taken the ring out of his jacket pocket. "Will you marry me,

Opal Elizabeth King?" he had asked. "Oh yes!" was her immediate answer. He had bruised her mouth when he kissed her, hard, and then pulled away again. The intensity of his kiss knocked her off balance, and rendered her speechless for several minutes—an intensity as great as the subsequent coolness when, after reciting Robbie Burns's "My Love is Like a Red, Red Rose" from memory, he walked off alone along the riverbank. It was as though he had merely forgotten—or was it had become?—himself for those few passionate moments, and then remembered how he wished to remain viewed by his future wife, his *fiancée*, and the world. But in her opinion he had shown her a piece of his heart; she knew he cared for her deeply even if he was so cautious about its expression.

Miscellaneous Shower for Bride-to-Be

Miss Opal Elizabeth King was the recipient of many pretty gifts at a miscellaneous shower given in her honour on Sunday afternoon. The reception room where the guests were welcomed was decorated with purple lilacs. In the tea room, lily of the valley centred the table where Mrs. Edward Poskitt presided over the tea cups. Miss Rose Greenham cut the ices. Little Miss Elsie Trick attended the door. The gifts were placed in a smartly trimmed basket which Miss Elsie presented to the bride-elect.

Her life since the announcement of their engagement was filled primarily with the topics Mac abhorred, and employed the very kind of language he had no use for, so at first she had been uncertain how much to tell him about all the showers and parties when she sat down to write. She had wanted to include him in what was going on in his absence, and had made one or two attempts to tell him about the festivities in their honour, conveyed in words that would suit him, but she soon gave up. Anyway, he told her flat out in his first response that he was genuinely uninterested in these "female activities." She had despaired at his blunt words. Her mother consoled, "Men sometimes have strange opinions on what is important. Other things occupy their minds." And Mac hadn't been *completely* brusque with her, had he? Well, yes, he had. He had said she could keep the stories for later—to tell her daughter, he said. So she wrote about the weather, and the family hardware store, and what her brothers had caught or shot, and left out the showers and dresses and flowers, and was careful not to open her heart too much.

Yet she continued to wish that he wrote back more often, and that he might occasionally add even a smidgen of romance, or some indication that he missed her. And that his letters weren't quite so full of legal anecdotes and weather reports. Phooey! Thankfully, she had plenty of thoughts of her own to fill her head. There was so much in the way of preparation for the wedding, so much in the way of showers and parties, and she was at the centre of them all. Just planning what to wear occupied considerable time.

Kitchen Shower for Bride-to-Be

The Misses Nettie and Ruby Lough, 129 Sherbrooke Street, were hostesses at a kitchen shower this after-

noon given in honour of Miss Opal King. A wedding ring hung from the chandelier, pink and white carnations centred the table, and four vases of lilies of the valley decorated the table corners. The Misses Lillie and Pearl King, and Mrs. R.F. Lough attended to the wants of the guests.

Opal Elizabeth was the eldest child of Georgetta and Reginald King, proprietors of King Hardware at 666 Main Street, Winnipeg. The Kings had seven children: Opal, 25, Lillie, 23, Reggie, 21, Pearly K, 19, Farley, 17, Melville, 14, and little Jimmy, 12. Lillie had just finished her third year at university. Reggie had entered law. Farley was finishing high school and working at the hardware store. Melville and Jimmy were both still in school, though Melville, who had never been quite right in the head, seldom made it into the classroom and likely wouldn't make it through another school year. His favourite pastime was picking fights with Pearly K—they were like oil and water, their mother said—though Pearly K was in no mood to fight with anyone these days. She'd left home on the train to make her way in the world with a government job in Ottawa, but within a month the MP she worked for had made inappropriate advances, and she had come back home. Since then she spent most of her time locked in her bedroom crying and writing poems she wouldn't share and that Melville tried unsuccessfully to find.

Georgie was from what Reg referred to as a "good family" in Truro. She considered herself a progressive woman, and her husband liked to say that she was "a woman of remarkable intelligence and vision," while he himself, being from, he said, lesser Oshawa stock, felt lucky to have married her. As far as Opal knew, only one issue had ever caused a serious disagreement between her parents, and that issue had first involved her. Georgie believed that her daughters had every right to be at university if the desire was there and the means were available. As that was the case, she expected Opal, as the eldest, to go first, and Opal badly wanted to. But Reginald King said no. He tried to explain. Education beyond the basics for women was a waste of time. He couldn't name a friend or acquaintance who thought otherwise. He loved his daughters dearly, but he was a businessman. "You don't invest in something that isn't going to pay you something in return," he told his wife. "You'd be thought a fool. I don't sell things in the store that are no use to anyone, now, do I? We'd be out of business in no time if I did." However, he added, in an attempt to smooth waters that were clearly roiling, his intention was that their three lovely daughters could and would be as happy as he could make them. He would make sure of it. All three were attractive and bright, and they would marry well. "Therefore," he said—holding up his hand to stop the objections about to burst from his wife's lips about daughters not being crates of nails or screws—"they *do not need to go to university*." The wiser choice was spending the money sending Reginald to study law, and then perhaps the other sons—excepting Melville, of course—should they evince a desire to do other than continue in the business with him, which he hoped Farley would do, and perhaps little Jimmy too, later on. Melville would always have employment stocking the shelves, sweeping and generally helping out.

Meanwhile, Reginald had had a good year and the girls could get one or two extra new dresses each, and more new shoes, and the sorts of gewgaws girls liked.

Georgie was angry and the air was cooler in the house for many months. But Reginald did not budge, and after graduating high school Opal went to work as a secretary at Mr. Tupper's law firm. She did not want to be the cause of discord between her parents; she was more inclined to peacemaking than troublemaking, and stifled her disappointment. "It's all right," she told her mother. "I like working there."

"It is *not* all right," retorted Georgie.

When Lillie graduated from high school, Georgie asked her husband again. There was a warning in her voice along with the question. Reginald said no again. But after an abundance of thinly veiled threats from his normally warm and loving Georgie, and an atmosphere of considerable coolness that showed no sign of dissipating, supplemented by pleading by Opal on her sister's behalf, he finally relented enough to say that Lillie could go if the money did not come from him. So Georgie contributed, and Opal provided the balance from her salary.

What was turning out to be the frosting on the cake for Opal was that Lillie was far more socially than academically inclined. She did not like being the so-called lucky one, and she wriggled out from under the mantle of a crusader for "women's rights" whenever she could. She cut classes, slept in, forgot to study, and flirted. If she eventually scraped through with a degree, it would be a miracle. Tiny seeds of resentment were sown in Opal each time she witnessed Lillie's lack of appreciation for all that was being done for her. Still, she was the perfect sister to have around when there was a wedding—she was funny, and lively, and had such good ideas when it came to the parties.

China Shower for Bride-to-Be

Miss Opal Elizabeth King, a bride of early June, was the recipient of many pretty bits of china at a shower given in her honour this afternoon. A large basket was attractively trimmed with white ribbons, and the parcels wrapped in tissue paper were placed therein. The unwrapping, with the reading of messages from Miss King's many girl friends, formed an interesting part of the afternoon's entertainment. The reception room was decorated with yellow tulips. The hostess wore a gown of black charmeuse with silk net tunic, the bodice of variegated chiffon. Miss King was wearing a smart costume of rose satin, with white ninon sleeves, and collar prettily trimmed with French embroidery. In the tea room the table was centred with red tulips. Mrs. Harry Johnson poured tea. Miss Lillie King cut the ices. Assisting were Misses Leta and Myrtle White, and Miss Pearl King.

Opal suspected that Mac's home life and growing-up years in Scotland hadn't been the happiest, but he was close-mouthed about his family. He had told her the basics—that his mother and father were still living in Thornhill; that he had a brother nine years younger, and two older sisters, both married. But beyond that he would not go. Only once did he mention that his elder sister, Joan, had married "badly," but when Opal asked for more, he would not elaborate.

As their wedding plans progressed, Mac did tell her that he had written to his family in Scotland to inform them of the impending marriage, but he cautioned that she should not expect to hear from them. Also, he said quickly, they were poor: she should expect no gift. "Oh, I hadn't!" she said, mortified. "I expect nothing at all!"

When Opal telephoned Mac in Calgary with the exciting news that she had received a letter from his mother, she was broadsided when Mac immediately flew into a murderous rage. He yelled at her into the telephone. How *dare* his mother interfere with his plans. How *dare* his mother stick her oar in where it was not wanted. On the other end, Opal felt faint, felt ill, so surprised was she at the hatred in his voice that she dropped the receiver. And when, picking it up again with trembling hands, she tried to break in to explain to him that the letter had been such a *nice* letter, he refused to listen, refused to let her speak as he continued to shout, and then turned his fury on her. Of *course* Opal could not see what the problem was, he sneered. Of *course* she would take his mother's part. That was a *female* for you. He spat the words angrily. He demanded that she forward the letter. Sobbing, she promised.

After hanging up the phone, she collapsed on the carpet in the hallway, where her mother found her. It was three days before she could mail the letter to Mac, because she had gone straight to bed. She had never been spoken to like that. No one she knew spoke like that. And she didn't understand, she didn't *understand*—the letter was just a letter, a nice, warm letter of welcome.

April 2, 1915
My dear Opal Elizabeth,

In this, my letter of greeting and welcome to you, on the eve of your becoming one of us, I have intentionally dispensed with any formality, and will therefore seek no excuse for the form of my address, and greet you in terms that I would a daughter, for is that not the position you are about to assume? To do otherwise would seem to me strangely not in keeping with the spirit in which this letter is written, nor would you, after reading it, take away the promise and feeling of a warm, and kindly reception, which I do here extend to you, and which spirit I am so desirous this letter should breathe throughout.

To compliment you upon the happy event which is about to take place, would be out of place here: your combined good sense and personal knowledge of one another necessarily dispense with the need of remarks upon my part. Sufficient is it for me to say, that the qualities which have proved James to be a good son, and an excellent brother, give good promise of the future.

Nor, indeed, will it be necessary for me to define any position for myself, or for the others. United, as a family, in the past, we have always been, united, in the present, we are, and for the future, we must remain so. Intermingled, in our lives, has been the loving desire to aid one another, in weel, in woe, and such, you will find, will be our desire, my dear future daughter, in the years that lie before us, when you will become one of our number.

Finally, I extend to you a mother's love, and with that, my duty is done.

In conclusion, I would sign myself if not as yet, then, in the future, my dear daughter,

Yours affectionately,
Mother—Margaret Graham Macaulay

Mac would later confide in her (without letting his eyes meet hers—his eyes skittered off her shoulder, and down onto the knees of his trousers, and the floor, and then back up to the cameo at her neck) about his relationship with his mother. Opal stayed still as he spoke, didn't move a muscle lest he stop, lest the slightest movement interrupt this fragile, rare intimacy. "My mother's primary occupation," he told her, "was getting me, her elder son, educated; she was that desperate that I should escape the poverty we lived in. She saw to it that I stuck to my books, and to that end she kept a whip handy."

Opal was horrified. A whip! He continued. It had been his mother's idea from the day he was born that he should go to Edinburgh University and become a lawyer, and she never let him forget what she expected of him. If he forgot everything else in his life, he said, he would not forget the look of grim determination on his mother's face as she refused him affection and denied him indulgence. He recalled that as a child he had brought her treasures he found on his walks. Flowers. Pebbles. Yet nothing was ever enough for her, or right, and she had hit the flowers from his hands.

"I am unable to think of her," he said, "without choking in anger." As he had on the telephone. She might remember that time.

"Yes," she said. But was his mother *always* unkind? she dared ask. Was she *never* good to him?

"Not that I recall," he said. "My father was the one for kindness, not her, and she held him in contempt for it. She was always unreasonable," he went on, words tumbling irregularly now from his mouth as he unburdened himself. "*Always.* I would have tried my best to please her," he said angrily, pain in his voice. "I didn't need her constant threats." After he dutifully finished law school, he had gone home to Thornhill one last time, to tell his parents his news: he was leaving for Canada. His father had looked sad, but had wished him well.

"And your mother?" asked Opal.

"If revenge were sweet," he said, "it should have been candy-coated by the look on her face when I told her. For once, she could barely speak." Mac chuckled bitterly. But that didn't last long. Soon enough, she had found voice, and told him he couldn't go, she wouldn't allow it. She told him she would not contribute a penny to his leaving Scotland. "I told her I had never expected her to contribute." And that was the end of that.

Poor Mac. Opal felt melancholy as she undressed for bed and brushed her thick brown hair a hundred strokes before plaiting it into a braid. She would be gentle, and kind, and a good wife to him. She pledged that he would always feel loved with her.

She slipped her nightgown on over her head and slipped off her slippers. She was feeling a little anxious, because lately Mac was becoming less and less real to her. He needed to appear, to confirm for her and the world that he was the flesh-and-blood man she had fallen so deeply in love with, and he with her. Really, all she wanted now was to be alone with him, away from the limelight that was claiming so much of her. Some days the stream of celebrations seemed more like hurdles and duties and less like fun, there were so many of them. And over the past few months doubt had been creeping more often into her thoughts. What if he no longer loved her? What if he didn't come? What if he abandoned her and stayed in Calgary and never gave her another thought and she was made an utter and complete fool of like Pearly K had been, only much, much worse?

She stood before her mirror with her hands on her hips, turning herself sideways and back, and thinking about Mac and hoping he would like what he saw. She had found herself wondering more and more about the physical part of married life. How was she going to manage? was what she was thinking, meaning the making of children, and all that went with it. The most intimate details of married life. Allowing him to put *that* in her—what would *that* be like? Putting his body against her body. Perhaps they would at some point be completely naked. The thought of his seeing her, and her him, made her blush deeply with embarrassment. She didn't really know what "it" on a man looked like, let alone how it would feel inside her. Would it be pointy like his nose, or cute and pudgy like a baby boy's? She had bathed her little brothers, but a man—she had never seen a man's. Would it feel strange? Repulsive? She was both excited and afraid.

Opal knelt beside her bed and said her prayers. Then she climbed into bed, where she recalled, as she always did before sleep, Mac's few short, hard kisses, the occasional touches of their hands, and their betrothal day on the riverbank. He *was* romantic. He *did* love her, he *must*, and she was foolish to doubt it. But the small store of memories she carried in her heart was getting worn from too much handling. She sighed, and turned out the bedside light.

Lying in her bed, Opal thought about the chest of silver that had arrived by train that afternoon from her mother's family in Truro. Her father had made a special trip home from the hardware store to bring it to her. She herself had used the clawed hammer to open the crate, and she and her mother had hoisted the chest up onto the dining room table. Now she imagined herself setting the table for their dinner together each night. The silver gleamed, the crystal sparkled. She pretended she was meeting him at the door when he came home from work, taking her apron off and laying it aside. He would take her in his arms and smile, then kiss her in greeting. She saw them dining together by candlelight, and then sitting companionably together before the fireplace the way her parents often did. She smiled a sleepy smile. Their marriage would be at least as long, she predicted, as her parents' was, and as happy.

Bride-elect Receives Clock

Last Monday evening the choir of Zion Methodist church met at the home of Mr. and Mrs. A. Monkman. Mr. Stanley Osborne, choir master, read the address,

and Mrs. Monkman presented Miss Opal King, a bride-elect of next week, with a beautiful brass clock from the choir. The rooms were decorated for the occasion with marguerites. Miss Phene Rowden and Miss S. Monkman assisted in serving the refreshments.

Soon! Mac would be here soon! He was on the way, he was on the train right this minute, coming to her. Opal stood in the dining room doorway picturing what he would see when he stood here right beside her. Last night she and Lillie had arranged the wedding and engagement gifts on the sideboard and the table—so many lovely presents to help her and Mac build their home together. The clock was on the mantel. She had placed the pretty silver teapot that had arrived from Mac's family in a place of honour in the centre of the dining room table. She loved the teapot's low-slung body, its ebony handle and graceful spout. It was the first thing she wanted Mac to see when today, yes today, in only an hour, he arrived in Winnipeg for their wedding. Finally! This time—the teapot time—she had written, not telephoned, the news that a present had come from his brother Michael on behalf of the family.

When they returned home from the train station, she took Mac's hat and coat, hung them up, then tried to take his hand to lead him, but he pulled back and away from her. "I'm coming," he said, "but I'll take my own time." She felt shame flush through her. He hadn't so much as touched her arm since he arrived, while she—she had longed to hug him, hard, to bury her face in his chest, to feel his arms around her. Instead she felt bereft, a fool.

Wedding Announcement

On Wednesday evening, June 9th, at 8 o'clock, in Zion Methodist church, the marriage of the daughter of Mr. and Mrs. Reginald King, to James Macaulay, M.A., LL.B., of Calgary, will take place. Miss Lillie King, sister of the bride, will be bridesmaid, Miss Norma Johnson, flower girl, and Mr. John Allen, best man.

"It looks like Christmastime in here," Mac said, and turned towards the fireplace where her father was standing. "But where is the tree? Where is the 'blazing Yule before us'?"

"Oh, you are funny! It's June!" Then, "Mac?" She tried to sound cheerful. "Come and see!" Reluctantly, he allowed her to steer him towards the table. "Look! Isn't it lovely?"

He didn't pick up the teapot. He moved to the sideboard instead, where he opened the lid of the chest of silver then closed it again. "Very nice," he said.

"But Mac, do you like the teapot?" She had picked it up and held it out to him.

"It's a nice enough piece, I suppose. It must have set them back."

She gave him the letter, and that was all, until she was bringing in a lunch tray and caught him putting the teapot down.

May 7, 1915
My dearest James,

In accordance with an old and invariable custom, it is the habit for all relatives and friends to mark the occasion of such an auspicious event as an impending wedding with a gift—a mark of esteem—if not also partaking of the nature of a remembrance of former happy days, before you left us to go to Canada. Nor would I desire, at this time, to be an exception to the general rule. Would you therefore accept of a present, sent by me on behalf of all our family, which I trust will reach you safely, accompanied, as it is, with all the best wishes that one brother could entertain for the other, and with the hope that it may long serve to grace the table of your future home.

More need not be said at this juncture—feelings rest in the heart, and have only their echo in words, but if sincere and heartfelt wishes for your health and prosperity in the married state may express to you my utmost desires at the present moment, then I am content, and can truly sign myself,

Ever your affectionate brother, Michael Edward Macaulay

Later that evening, at the dinner table, dabbing lemon meringue from his mouth with his serviette, Mac said, "I should perhaps mention something."

He was in good humour, Opal was glad to see; he must have liked his brother's letter, he must like the teapot, for before dinner he had taken her aside and kissed her, tenderly.

"I have purchased something for you, Opal. Which I hope will bring you pleasure while you are home alone while I am at work." He looked at her across the table.

"Yes?" She couldn't keep the excitement out of her voice.

"I have acquired for you," he said, "a piano."

"Mac!" Opal burst into tears. All her hopes and fears of the last few weeks and all the panic inside her collapsed. The kiss, and now this. She cried openly in joy and relief. "Mac! Mac!" What a ninny she had been for doubting him. For her fleeting loss of faith in him.

There was no doubt that Mac was pleased to have pleased her, in spite of his evident discomfort at the emotional outburst. "It's a grand piano," he added. "A small one, but good quality. German." He raised his hand. "I know, I know. The war. But you can't deny they make good pianos."

"Get hold of yourself, Opal," said her father.

"Yes, pull yourself together, Opal," said her mother disapprovingly, her eyes smiling. Lillie and Pearly K were both grinning now.

Melville was rolling his eyes. "Now you'll have to learn to play decently, sis."

"She already *knows*," retorted Pearly K. "She plays beautifully."

"Beautifully for a rhinoceros," giggled Melville.

Lillie kicked Opal's chair. Jimmy laughed into his glass and spilled his milk.

"I have heard her play quite nicely," said Mac.

"Well, Mac, that is quite the *grand* gesture," quipped Reginald, and everyone groaned.

But there was more, and Mac made his biggest announcement while the wave of excitement over the piano had not yet ebbed. "I have made another purchase as well," he said, regaining their attention. "Somewhere to keep the piano. I have purchased . . . a house."

Opal, Lillie, Pearly K and even Georgie gave squeals, while the men and boys made deeper sounds of pleasure. Reginald and Georgie exchanged smiles, and looks. They were impressed. First that diamond ring, and then the piano, and now this.

"A house?" Opal exclaimed, sitting back down in astonishment. *"A house!"*

Yes, a house. It was situated just a block from the Elbow River, he told them, and conveniently close to a new school where their future children might go (Opal blushed). The house was a brown bungalow with white trim and a green shingled roof. Here—he would show them a photograph. As they could see, if they gathered round, a large veranda ran across the front, and half of it was glassed in for protection from the weather. The style of the house was unfamiliar to both Opal and her parents. The style, said Mac, reflected the characters of its original owners, an Englishman and his French wife. In the picture, Mac was standing on the front steps, wearing a suit and a boater, arms akimbo, proud.

June 15, 1915

Mrs. James Macaulay, née Opal King, of Winnipeg, greeted a large number of guests at the tea house yesterday, on the occasion of her first reception since her marriage. She wore her wedding gown of duchesse satin, with court train and trimmings of shadow lace. Receiving with her was Mrs. J. Deslisle May, who was wearing her wedding gown of ivory charmeuse, trimmed with duchess lace, and Mrs. Johnson, of Winnipeg, who was wearing her wedding gown of pink and white voile with shadow lace.

The tea room appointments were carried out in yellow and green, the table centred with a basket of yellow mums, swathed in yellow tulle. Mrs. George May and Mrs. D.T. Townsend shared the honours the first hour, and were later relieved by Mrs. Kiteley and Mrs. George M. Thompson. Miss Helen and Miss Genevieve Thompson waited on the door.

Opal found the clackety-clack of the train as it headed west unnerving, though it didn't seem to bother Mac, head buried deep in his thick books. She did needlework to pass the time, but she had done so much of it in the last two years that it brought her very little pleasure or sense of purpose anymore. She had finished reading her books, *Aunt Jane's Nieces Out West* and *O Pioneers!*, both travelling gifts from her sisters, as well as *The Return of Tarzan*, courtesy of Farley. (It's a loaner not a keeper, he said.) Her hands sat uselessly in her lap. She wanted to wring them. What else was there to make? Mac's suitcase was half filled with handkerchiefs, and it was early to start on baby things, not to mention bad luck.

Eventually she started feeling a little pouty. Neglected. This was, after all, their honeymoon, wasn't it? She shifted slightly. She was sore down there, but not unpleasantly. She changed her train of thought. She tried to yet again entertain herself by thinking about their house, and how she would decorate it, but this daydream went only so far when all she had seen was a photograph of the outside. Having never been to Calgary, she found it impossible to imagine the location. This morning at breakfast she had tried teasing Mac into giving her more particulars, but he wouldn't tell her a thing. "It's a surprise," he said. "You'll see it soon enough." Still she pestered, until he burst out unkindly, "You'll see it when you see it. Shut your trap, would you?" Heads turned in the dining car and she was ashamed.

So she held the photograph and pictured the inside of the house herself. She pictured the front door opening, and Mac carrying her, his beloved bride, over the threshold. She saw the house as completely empty but for the trunks and crates that had arrived in their absence and were stacked in the foyer and living room waiting for her. The house echoed slightly with their footsteps. Light streamed through the windows. In the foyer Opal saw herself turning her head towards the living room, where she saw for the first time the grand piano Mac had bought as his wedding present to her. In her mind the piano was standing alone in its grandeur, gleaming in afternoon light. Dear Mac. How had he known buying the piano would make her so happy? And how had he, not a particularly musical person, chosen it?

Still he read. She sighed heavily. She might as well be by herself for all the attention he paid her, the old bookworm. He didn't notice, or pretended he didn't notice, her small ploys for attention. Difficulty getting a hat box down. Difficulty opening the compartment door. She could be murdered and thrown off the train by robbers and he wouldn't notice until dinnertime. Opal picked one of Mac's books from the pile—pages like tissue paper, and written in Greek. Another in Latin. Politics. History. Biography. Nothing, he looked up to say, suitable for a woman to read. Well, what did he think she was to do while he did all that reading? she wondered to herself. Stare out the window forever? She did have a brain she would like the opportunity to use, if only in conversation. Was that so much to ask?

Opal did smile as Mac carried her over the threshold of her new Calgary home. But as soon as he set her down in the foyer, she looked around completely baffled. Whose was all this furniture? Puzzled, she looked at Mac, who was uncharacteristically grinning from ear to ear. Pictures and curtains, furniture, lamps, carpets and doilies—whose house was this? Without moving, she looked around her.

"Mac? Whose house is this?"

"Well, it's yours, of course."

And then he told her the rest of the story. An Englishman and his bride, a Frenchwoman, had, as he had told her in Winnipeg, built this house five years before. The Frenchwoman had had no particular love for Canada, but since she was so terribly in love with her debonair husband, she had agreed to settle in "the colonies." But then, without warning, the Englishman died, and the Frenchwoman wanted to flee this *très mauvais* country as fast as she could and return to France. So Mac had seized the opportunity—*carpe diem!*—and bought this house completely furnished, right down to the tea towels in the kitchen and right up to the grand piano in the living room. Opal wouldn't have to do a thing except unpack her clothes, he crowed.

"Why didn't you tell me?" she asked him, her throat so constricted she could barely speak.

"It wouldn't have been much of a surprise if I had told you, would it?" Things were not unfolding as he had imagined they would. And whose fault was that? He strode over to the sideboard to pour himself a Scotch. He got out a glass. The decanter.

"Mac! What do you think you're doing?"

"I'm taking a drink."

"Mac! You promised me. You *promised* me not to drink in our home! We haven't been here an hour!"

Mac took up the decanter and held it tight against his chest like a child with a doll. "Go to hell," he said, glaring at her. Then he took up the glass and went out to the garage.

Opal sobbed as she walked from room to room looking at the elegant furniture—the intricately carved living room pieces upholstered in rose-coloured jacquard; the china cabinet and long sideboard; the large circular dining table with carved claw legs and the eight matching chairs upholstered in dark blue velvet. Upstairs, the Italian walnut bedroom suite, the pale green and yellow satin duvets on the beds, the thick white towels in the bathroom. Every drawer and cupboard she opened was filled. In spite of its obvious quality, there was nothing—nothing—she would have chosen herself. She sat down on the landing and cried.

She could have packed away the woman's towels, and sheets, and linens, but she didn't, and for years she would feel she was snooping through another woman's house. She left her own things packed in their crates and boxes, and had the maid, once she'd hired one through the YWCA employment services, help her move them down the narrow wooden stairs into the basement.

And so she tried to acclimatize, and succeeded somewhat. Once she knew her house better she relaxed a bit, and while Mac was at work she set herself to learning to play the music for the song version of "My Love is Like a Red Red Rose" for him. To show him she had forgiven him for not telling her about the house; to try to get them on an even keel.

"Sit down," she told him a few weeks later with a smile when he came home. "I have a surprise for you."

But it wasn't a good day for romance: Mac's work that day had been difficult. He had been wrangling with plans for the railway, and what he had hoped would take an hour or two had taken the whole day. After stopping in the garage for a drink, what he craved now more than anything was some supper and some time to himself, not some female malarkey. But to please her he sat down and appeared to listen. He stood up the moment she finished and said, "Very nice. Thank you." And as he left the room, he turned to say, "I bought you the piano for your *own* pleasure, not mine. I'll thank you not to play while I'm here."

And that was the kind of daily exchange that occurred in the life they settled into. Every day Mac went out into the world and then came back to the house again at night via the garage. Opal adapted as best she could to her husband's wants, but she never felt secure. His lack of physical and verbal affection made her suspect early on that he simply didn't like her; it seemed to her as though he had *expected* to be disappointed by her, but she didn't know why. She had always considered herself, and thought others considered her, a good person. She had never questioned herself. But now she began to ask herself what was *wrong* with her. And why had he married her if he didn't like her? It made no sense. Nor did the times he behaved as though it were *she* who didn't like *him*. The unfairness with which she felt he treated her made her chronically worried, and stubbornly certain he was wrong in his opinion of her, while she also began fearing that he was right. Eventually she became a little snappy herself. And then more. She gradually changed until she didn't always recognize herself; she started to doubt things that she had never spent a breath on before. Perhaps, it occurred to her one day, she had deformities of person or personality that only *she* could not see, and that her own family had loved her too much ever to point out. It was such a gradual and subtle erosion of her confidence that she barely noticed it; it was as though her self-esteem were a bar of rosewater soap run under warm water for hours on end.

Little Pearl's hair was straight and black and her dark brown eyes were like Opal's brother Farley's and her sister Pearly K's, while baby May had her mother's larger bones and plump softness. May's wavy hair was light brown, and she would have fair and freckled Scottish skin and blue eyes, and though her smile would become self-conscious, it was both warm and tolerant, even when her big sister, whom she adored, treated her unkindly.

Both daughters were born at home, Pearl in 1917, May in 1921. The first time Pearl saw May, Pearl had shyly, even softly, approached the bassinet where her new baby sister lay. Pearl peeked in and took one look at May, and a wail rose from inside her and grew in volume as she stamped out of the room, up the stairs and slammed her bedroom door. Not only did her new sister have the only blue eyes in the family, she sobbed to Opal when she coaxed and coaxed her to divulge what was wrong, but now Pearl would have to *share.* Everything. Everything that mattered, everything that had been all hers until this interloper had arrived. When a smile played on Opal's lips, little Pearl had looked at her with adult fury and ordered her mother out of her room. Opal had gone.

Pearl was a strange child, and Opal was intimidated by her. When Opal knelt and embraced her, Pearl stood stiff as a stick, offering little or nothing in return. Pearl's rare smiles always seemed forced, and laced with unhappiness. What appeared to Opal to be an inherent sadness that she had seen early on in her little girl's face had almost broken her heart. But as Pearl grew older, the sadness gradually became a fixed expression that more closely resembled displeasure as Pearl became, apparently, chronically dissatisfied and cranky. Nothing and no one could please her, and that's how she stayed. In some ways, Pearl was a lot, Opal thought, like Mac. Like him, her gaze was shrewd and somewhat unnerving; even when she was very young she had looked suspicious, as if someone somewhere was getting something that she was not, or that something was going on that she ought to be privy to and wasn't. Something wasn't fair. How to convince her beloved daughter that the world had other things on its mind than thwarting her every desire? If Pearl liked *them* better, people would like *her* better, she told her. People were offended when other people did not trust them. But Pearl did not care.

She could stay mad for days, refusing to speak or even acknowledge anyone's existence. Yet Opal had heard desperate sobs emanating from Pearl's room, had heard her daughter's weeping and wailing that no one loved her, so she knew Pearl was not without feelings. But she would not open her door to her mother, and to her father only when he angrily demanded that she do so or he'd thrash her.

Pearl could stay mad at her sister for days, refusing to speak to her or even acknowledge her existence. If little May looked sad or hurt, Pearl ignored her. She treated her sister like a curse that had been sent to interfere with the way the world should run—which was, of course, around Pearl. Little May would traipse after her looking so unhappy it would melt anyone's heart but Pearl's. Pearl slammed the door in her face. "That girl had better learn that's not the way things work!" said Mac, as he locked Pearl in her room for insolence. "She may speak to you rudely, but I won't put up with it. Let her stew. She'll sort herself out soon enough."

Mac had strict rules about many things, and required Opal to enforce them when he was not present. Discipline was a mother's job, he said, implying when they misbehaved that Opal wasn't fulfilling her responsibilities. Mac might administer verbal chastising, but he would not administer corporal punishment, though he considered it necessary. Let them hate their mother, not him, thought Opal. The children were not allowed in the parlour unless they wanted to practise on the piano or there was company. They were to keep their hands off the furniture because Mac didn't like fingerprints on everything and the maid had better things to do than to run around cleaning up after them. They were to keep their feet off the clawed feet of the dining room table because it scuffed the wood and made an annoying sound. They were, as was the accepted wisdom, to be seen and not heard. Period.

Opal didn't like to hit her daughters. Her own parents had never hit their children, had admonished them with quiet, stern words when it was necessary, which hadn't been often. Her father had only once raised his hand to the boys, and the occasion was so unusual that Melville had been just as surprised as their father. But Opal did what Mac told her to do with Pearl, hitting her either with her hands or with a stick Mac acquired and gave her expressly for the purpose, and then Opal cried for hours afterwards, torn by the pull between being an obedient wife and a loving mother. Without her husband's permission, she lightened the touch with May.

Summer holidays usually involved a week or two in a cabin in Banff, and two weeks for the girls riding horses at the King Ranch in Millarville. But in the summer of 1926, the Macaulays took a sea voyage to Britain. It was the first time Mac had been back home, which he regretted deeply, as his father had died in January without ever seeing his grandchildren. Pearl was nine, May five when they embarked. The twenties were turning out to be the best decade of their lives together. Mac had prospered, and he didn't mind showing his mother that was the case, with the clothes he dressed his family in, and the manner in which they travelled and lodged. First they went to London, where they visited the Tower and Buckingham Palace, and then they hired a car and driver and went north to Scotland. The week they spent there with his mother was tense and unpleasant, and the absence of his father and the presence of his mother created a turmoil in Mac that resulted, Opal could see, in his hardening himself like shellac. Which made it difficult for everyone, his mother included. He could barely speak a civil word.

As they travelled south into England again, Mac decided that he wanted to have his sister Joan meet his children and his wife. How many years had it been? Almost twenty, surely. His sister had married badly, he reminded Opal, and this time he gave her the details. She had married an Indian doctor named Walla who was from Bombay, of all places, in spite of her family's forbidding it. Now, he said, he had changed his mind about it all. Surely there were worse things than marrying a coloured man, and if they visited during the daytime he would not have to set eyes on him. He wanted his sister to see that he was doing well; he wanted her to be pleased for him the way she had tried on occasion to be when he was a child, removing him sometimes from their mother's path, from her grasp. So when they arrived back in London, he took Opal, Pearl and May to his sister's door, and brusquely knocked with short, hard raps. Joan opened the door. When she saw who it was, an indescribable look swept across her face. Then she closed the door in her brother's face. Not only that, but she had caught her skirt in the door, and had to open and shut it *again.*

Mac looked dumbstruck, crushed, and then his face went hard. As hard and as black, Opal thought, as that day he came out of Mr. Tupper's office. He ordered his family away, and walked apart from them back to the hotel. He remained ill-tempered even when they had crossed the Channel to France, and in Paris, where Opal bought her mother and each of her sisters a dress, Mac, still smarting from his sister's rebuff, was vocal in his disapproval of the expenditure, and there in their hotel room they fought.

"You make too much of that family of yours," he said.

"I do not," she said.

"You are completely foolish when it comes to them. You'd think you hadn't a brain in your head."

"Fiddle-dee-dee. I am not. And I do so." Then she recklessly added, "Well, at least I talk to my family."

She and Mac didn't speak to each other for days after that, and they said to their two daughters, *Tell your mother this. Tell your father that,* though May was the only one to co-operate. Pearl sat staring at the wall or the floor, sullen and silent, ignoring them all. "I refuse to partake in such idiocy," she said finally, in a very grown-up voice.

On the day the Supreme Court of Canada ruled against the Alberta Five, saying that women were not persons, Opal had gritted her teeth and barely held her tongue while Mac, jubilant, crowed at the dinner table as he sat with his wife and daughters and the maid waited on the table. He said to them that anyone with a brain knew already that women should not serve in the Senate. He said these females had wasted the court's time, anyone could see that. This was the culmination of many months of one-sided "discussions" on the topic: Mac had spoken often and long about it. Women were too stupid to see that they were out of their league wanting such rights. He needed to look no further than his own wife with her willy-nilly spending habits if he wanted to see a woman in action. There were female pursuits and male pursuits. Women excelled at their chosen activities, and men at theirs. What was so hard to understand about that? Opal sat across from her husband and watched her daughters absorb his words.

But that wasn't the end of it. They were subjected to more of Mac's rants on the topic a year and a half later when, on October 18, 1929, England's Privy Council overturned the Supreme Court's ruling. Now Mac was disgusted, criticized his supper, and announced (Finally! thought Opal) that the topic was permanently closed.

Like her own mother, Opal prided herself on being well informed. She had followed the course of justice with interest, and had read all the newspaper articles on the subject, secretly cheering the women on. She was determined that when they grew up her own daughters would be considered persons, and that they both would go to university; she was determined to have more success than her own mother had had trying to educate her daughters—it was a whole generation later. It was sinful not to train the mind God gave you, she told Mac, as Pearl drew closer to her high school graduation, and continuing with what Mac called Opal's "relentless harangue" on the subject. What good had educating her sister Lillie done? he said, presenting yet again his favourite piece of evidence. Hadn't Opal spent all that time and money working at the law firm as a secretary so that her sister could go to university? And while Lillie had finished—just barely—she never actually did a thing with her teaching degree. Lillie had promptly married a wealthy man, hadn't she, and didn't have to lift a finger in the way of work unless she wanted to. It was in being a homemaker and socialite that Lillie excelled, not intellectual pursuits. Lillie herself had known that, and Opal should have too, instead of wasting her money. If Lillie had married well in the first place, what would have been wrong with that? He, for one, had no money to waste. The thirties were not like the twenties: the whole country was in a Depression, she should remember.

Opal knew all too well. Mac and the papers provided them daily with statistics. Over a million Canadians were unemployed. The cost of living had sunk dramatically: in Calgary, eggs were three cents a dozen, a leg of lamb was $1.50. Milk was ten cents a quart. On Ninth Avenue, Mac said, you could purchase a breakfast of coffee, two slices of toast and butter, bacon and one egg for fifteen cents. In 1933, wheat had sold on the Liverpool market at thirty-three cents per bushel, the lowest price in three hundred years. And in the past two years Mac had taken two ten-percent cuts to his salary.

But then, within a matter of months, things had turned around, for the Macaulays at least. In November 1934, Mac was promoted to Chief Solicitor for Alberta. He bought May a bicycle for Christmas, Opal a new fur coat, himself a new car; and he promised Pearl a trip to Hawaii on a CPR steamer as her grade twelve graduation gift. Opal pressed harder for her daughters' education. Mac relented. But, he said, it would have to be McGill, the best Scottish Canadian university, or nothing.

Opal's youngest brother, Jimmy, had started out in the family hardware store but decided that he didn't much want to be bossed around by older brothers for the rest of his life. So he found himself a job as a tobacco salesman, which didn't please his parents much but did please his older brother Melville, who smoked like a chimney his whole life long. "I know what *I* want for Christmas, Jimmy!" he'd say with his huge and goofy laugh. "Some more of those tailor-made smokes you sell!" Jimmy turned out to be a good salesman. At first his sales territory was limited to northern Manitoba, but within two years he was transferred to Calgary, and said goodbye to his parents, and Melville, and his other siblings. As good luck would have it, Opal and Mac had recently moved up into Mount Royal and hadn't sold their first house yet, so Jimmy and his family rented it. Mac's only stipulation was that Jimmy wasn't to smoke in the house. "If I have to go outside for a drink, Opal, then he can step outside to smoke," he said. But of course Jimmy didn't.

Mabel Maude, Jimmy's wife, was Opal's favourite sister-in-law; Opal had always found her *utterly* charming. Effervescent, even, and so endlessly kind. Jimmy called her M&M, after those candies in the cardboard tubes that had just come out. *Everyone* liked her. Especially Melville—he and Jimmy had come close to blows over her more than once because of Melville's ridiculous attempts at flirting. When they were still dating, and even after they were married, Melville would put his arm around M&M, or tickle her until she giggled, or whisper in her ear, or lift her right up onto his shoulder, she was so little and he was so big. Melville knew that his moves drove Jimmy wild, and he always watched to see what kind of reaction he was getting. So then

Jimmy would stop supplying Melville with cigarettes, and Melville would get mad and pout and try to trip Jimmy every time he walked by his chair.

Opal knew that Jimmy had smoked now and again since he was in his teens and sneaked the odd one out of Melville's pack, but working for the tobacco company, it wasn't long before Jimmy was a heavier smoker than Melville—which was really saying something—and taking full advantage of the free cigarettes from the company. When Jimmy would go home to Winnipeg to visit head office or the family, Georgie told Opal, he and Melville would sit out on the porch together to smoke because she, Georgie, wouldn't have it in her house, and they were out there most of the day and into the night, immersed in the thick haze of smoke.

In Calgary, Jimmy's coughing had started to become a nuisance; his regular smoker's cough had gradually grown in both frequency and depth. He began to make such a hair-raising and unpleasant racket each morning as he spat out the phlegm and guck that poor horrified Mabel Maude ran the water in the kitchen sink until one of the children pulled at her skirt to tell her that he was finished. To the three little boys, the sounds their father made in the mornings would become ones they remembered as familiar, almost homey, and comforting in their ritual quality, and in the incremental repetition. The cough eventually grew so deep and so rich that it interfered with his breathing, and then his talking; he noticed it most, he told Opal, when he gave his selling spiel. He was still in his thirties when the verdict came down: cancer of the lung in both lungs. Still, he did not stop smoking, and everything in the house reeked of it, from the curtains to the towels to the children's socks and underwear. Too late now, he said ruefully, and put another cigarette between his lips and flicked open his years-of-service lighter.

With Pearl away at McGill and May in high school, Opal had time to help Mabel Maude with Jimmy as he grew sicker, and since the houses were less than a mile apart, it was convenient too, an easy walk down the hill from Mount Royal into Elbow Park, though returning home up the hill was another matter.

Each time she entered the house, Opal remembered that day in 1915 when Mac had carried her across this very threshold and put her down in this very foyer. She remembered in both her body and her mind how what had met her eyes had baffled and hurt her and caused their first serious fight. She had wondered since if they had ever really got over that fight: in some ways it seemed to have marred their entire life together. She shook her head at the recollection. If becoming a married woman weren't strange enough in and of itself—filled with the struggle to form a new identity first as wife and then as wife and mother, her own family left behind in Winnipeg—she had struggled also, struggled hard, and alone, and unappreciated, with living in an environment defined almost completely by a stranger's belongings. It hadn't been until they moved up the hill that her trousseau was completely unpacked. More than twenty-five years after the wedding, she finally felt she was *home.*

The living arrangements in the house were different now. Upstairs, the bedroom where Opal's two daughters had been born was now Jimmy's sickroom. Mabel Maude slept in what had been the maid's room. The three boys shared the master bedroom, their three single beds like lozenges in a row and inhabited by the eldest, Michael, and youngest, Jack (who wanted to be nearest the door), with Wilson in the middle.

Spring ended and with the start of summer Pearl returned home from McGill. A month later May graduated from high school. Opal attempted to engage both her daughters in helping their uncle and his family, not together, of course, since Pearl still despised her sister. May helped willingly, but Pearl, with her nose crammed in one book or another all the day long, obviously considered herself above all that pedestrian stuff like family, and she did not, she said plainly, like sickness. She did not, she said, like children. They were utterly annoying. "You might occasionally think beyond yourself," said Opal, a comment which fell, like most of her comments to Pearl, on deaf ears. In fact, all her words met with a stony silence that commented, it seemed to Opal, more on Opal's stupidity for asking than on Pearl's hardness of heart.

So sometimes with May but more often alone, Opal faced the slog back up the hill at the end of a long day of helping out. As she left Jimmy's house, turned right and began the climb, Opal reminded herself that she needed the exercise. Like her own mother, she tended towards plumpness, and her fondness for pies and ice cream didn't help. Strawberry ice cream. Blackberry pies. Vanilla ice cream. May had inherited her mother's build, so she would have to watch out too when she got older, but the golf she played with her father had so far kept plumpness in check. Pearl was luckier: she would not have such a problem to struggle with. Pearl was compact, smaller-boned, sturdy, like her father. And hard. Headed. Hearted. Faced. Her struggles would be of a different order.

Funny, Opal thought as she trudged, how one child will inherit one aspect of a parent, another child another, and sometimes the combinations are complementary, sometimes not. The two girls were as light and dark in mood as they were fair and dark in hair and complexion. May was so easy to get along with. She did what she was told, and she came readily to her mother for affection. Pearl stood to one side and glared balefully, as though she had been refused affection before she had even sought it, which she seldom did.

As Opal felt her own heart pumping and her own lungs working harder and harder to provide her with the oxygen she needed to climb the last part of the hill, she thought of her brother Jimmy's lungs and how they couldn't hold enough air anymore, and how he'd never be able to make it up this hill, or any hill, ever again, and when she felt these waves of fear and despair, she felt tears welling in her eyes and wished again that Mac had come to get her in the car, especially on such a hot day. He was home from work by now. Didn't he know it was hard for her? Didn't he care? Opal stopped. Why did she bother asking? Mac didn't care about much, except perhaps Mac. And the way he got angry with himself for not landing a fish or for missing a golf shot suggested he didn't hold himself in the highest regard either. Pearl was her father's daughter, no doubt about that.

After she'd caught her breath, Opal stepped forward once again. She was perspiring; the day had been warm. By the time she came in the gate and front door of her own house, she was physically and emotionally exhausted, and she collapsed in a chair in the foyer. Mac would be upstairs, in his study, with the window opened wide and the electric fan going. When the maid—the new one, the one with the cyclone hair—came out of the kitchen, Opal asked for a glass of lemonade. She carried her cold drink out to the summer house, her favourite place, and sat down on the bench, and pushed the stray hairs off her hot, moist face, and sighed as she mopped her forehead and cheeks, and viewed the colourful gladioluses in her garden, all the while thinking about her little brother Jimmy, and Mabel Maude, and the three little boys. How wrong it was that he, the youngest of all the King children, was dying. She would remember him best and most as the dear little baby she had helped her mother with. That's how she saw him, that's how she would always see him, not as the grey and wasting man who lay dying in bed, wheezing and trying to cough.

Opal needed to talk about her brother's suffering. She needed to talk about his endless and terrible coughing, about the great gobs of black guck that he spat into the basin. She had broached the topic with Mac many times, until he had told her to shut her trap on that particular topic and keep it that way. So sensitive himself, she thought. But not when it came to the feelings of others. He had heard enough, he said peevishly. He had little sympathy for her brother: tobacco was a disgusting habit and anyone who took such poisonous stuff deserved what he caught from it. Mac hadn't seen his brother-in-law in over six months; he hadn't set foot in the house since Christmas, when he wouldn't shut his own trap about how much the house reeked of tobacco smoke. As if that mattered anyhow. The best he would do now was wait in the car out on the street if it was raining and lay on the horn to hurry her up when he was the one who was late.

So the only ones left to tell were her daughters, who *had* to stay in the same room with her if she insisted. Pearl sat hard and tense, staring at a spot on the floor while her mother spoke. May, soft and worried, held her hands clasped in her lap and nodded her head sympathetically. May was such good company; what was the matter with Pearl? Opal had never seen anyone so critical. From the word go, no one could do a blessed thing right in her eyes, and Opal wished to goodness she'd get over it, but she doubted she would.

The air of superiority with which Pearl had departed for McGill had returned with her in spades. Whenever Pearl was in the same room with her mother, everything in Pearl's body looked as though it wanted to leave, as though she couldn't get away from her mother fast enough. *Everything* Opal said was met with a look of contempt, *every* answer had been dipped in condescension. If looks could wither, Opal would be, she thought, a small pile of dried sage or raspberry leaves under a pestle. If they could kill, she would long be in the ground and forgotten. Compost for her flowers. And in the face of her daughter's intolerance during these lopsided conversations, and in some perverse if futile attempt to *make* her daughter stay long enough to love her, Opal became stubborn, as if keeping her daughter there long enough would change her mind, would make her *want* to spend time with her mother. But still Pearl's body leaned and pulled towards the doorway, which Pearl herself seemed not to notice, but Opal did, and went on talking even more, as if stopping would give Pearl the opportunity she longed for, but in her nervousness she would bungle the words and sound as stupid as Pearl believed her to be. If she stopped, Pearl would escape, and Opal would be alone with the terrible images of her brother dying, coupled with the knowledge that her own daughter so clearly disliked and maybe even hated her.

It was all bad in those days.

Staring at her spot on the floor, Pearl said nothing, but she undoubtedly heard every word, seethed inside, silently screamed at her mother to shut the *h-e*-double-*l* up, until eventually, finally, Opal wound down, and started to cry. Escape was at hand.

"May I go now, Mother?"

"You are heartless," Opal accused her, hating the whine in her voice. "You haven't been down to see your uncle since you got back. You haven't even called him on the telephone. And I thought you liked your aunt Mabel Maude. If not your little cousins."

"Your descriptions are so vivid, Mother, that I don't need to see them."

"They would like to see you."

"I detest smoking."

"I think you should go for a visit."

"Let May take my regards."

"Heartless," Opal said again.

Pearl looked at her coldly. Gave a huge, exasperated sigh. "I'll go with Dad. When *he* goes."

"Pearl—"

"Mother? I have art history to read. I ought to be through the Renaissance by now."

"Then go, you wretch!" Opal cried out angrily, gesturing with her hands to brush her daughter towards the door. "Go on. Get out of my sight. Don't make me look at you. Don't let me keep you from the blessed Renaissance."

Art history. English literature. As if Opal, because she had not gone to university, was therefore feeble-minded. As if her not going were a result of her own stupidity, not that of others. Well, it had not been her choice, she would have said if her daughter had cared to know. This daughter of hers knew nothing of her mother's struggles, her mother's thwarted desires, and likely wouldn't care anyway. Pearl had been handed her education on a silver platter, just as Lillie had been handed hers. After considerable work by Opal, the both of them. But at least Pearl took her education seriously. Too seriously, perhaps.

By the end of July, Jimmy no longer left the bedroom, and the sounds of his suffering permeated the walls of the house and wafted through the doorways and out the windows into easy earshot of the neighbours. Mabel Maude said that every window of the house had to be open day and night to ensure they didn't all roast to death, and to get fresh air, even hot fresh air, circulating inside the house.

Jimmy lay thin and pale and weak, barely able to cough. He had been such a big man, too big, in fact, for a long while after he and M&M married. She was even better than Opal with pies and cakes, and oh, how Jimmy had loved his coconut cream! And now he had wasted away to jutting bones and hollowed eyes, and he turned his face away from food. Mabel Maude had grown thin as a shadow as well; she was worn and tired all the time now. Opal brought her flowers from her garden, and the tall stalks of bright gladiolus blossoms resting against M&M's pale face as she cradled them like a baby made her look more grandmother than mother.

Opal came into Jimmy and Mabel Maude's the back way one morning to see how their garden was doing. As she passed the garage door, she smelled smoke. Tobacco smoke. She pushed open the garage's side door, and inside in the cool shadows she discovered Michael, not yet eight, waving his hands through the air in a futile attempt to disperse the smoke. Opal ran at him, smacked him around the head with her purse, smacked him while he ducked and wept, and then held him against her in the cool dark while his body shook with grief.

Jimmy died at the end of an unusually hot and humid August day. The boys were across the street fishing in the Elbow River. The two women sat beside his body, bathed in their own perspiration, tears and sweat coursing down their faces and between their breasts to their bellies.

As the family all left the house in Winnipeg together in their sombre grey and black funeral clothes, suits, dresses, coats and hats, in spite of the hot summer day, and filed past Melville in the porch where he sat in his favourite chair, he did not raise his head: he watched their feet as they went by. He was wearing his suit, but with a scarf of Pearly K's, red and white striped silk, tied in a bow around his neck.

"We thought you were getting ready to go, Mel," said Opal.

"Guess you thought wrong," he said.

"I didn't say you could wear my scarf," said Pearly K.

"Tough," said Melville. "I never asked if I could." He would not speak another word to anyone, just sat there hunched over, smoking and mumbling and smoking. He would smoke uncontrollably for days, Georgie told Opal, in his lap a carton of Jimmy's brand of cigarettes. He didn't use an ashtray, just ground out each butt on the porch floor with the heel of his boot after he had lit a fresh one.

Opal watched her elder daughter closely as Pearl approached the coffin at the front of the church, but no look of sadness or grief crossed her daughter's face. May snuffled and sobbed beside her mother. After standing at the coffin for about ten seconds, Pearl returned to the pew and sat down again. Opal kept watching her. How could anyone be so hard, so heartless?

Before the lid of the casket was closed, Mabel Maude approached the coffin with her three children one last time. She leaned into the coffin and kissed her husband goodbye. Her little sons were clustered around her, their bewildered faces full of sadness. One boy reached in and tried to hold his father's hand, but pulled away at the coldness and stiffness, and the look he gave in that split second was full of realization. Pearl's were surely the only dry eyes in the church as everyone watched this scene. Even the minister wept.

But when the church had been emptied of the living and the dead, Pearl couldn't be found to go with them to the interment, and Opal went back into the church to look for her. When she heard the sounds of sobbing and of moaning coming from inside the bathroom, she stopped outside the door. As she listened to the sounds of sorrow, a small but joy-filled smile of gratitude spread tentatively across her face, as though the sound of her daughter in anguish were a gift from God. Her daughter had a heart after all. Opal whispered a thank-you before she pushed open the bathroom door.

Inside, Pearl was leaning against the wall, her hot cheek against the small white tiles. Her shoulders slumped, she held herself in her arms as though she were in pain. Pearl's face was turned upwards, twisted and distorted, transfigured and wet, tears still streaming down her face. Opal approached her daughter tentatively, carefully, scrabbling to open her purse and get out a hanky, which she offered, saying, "Dear?" But when Pearl turned to her, the look on her face was instantly one of sheer hatred, and she hissed, "Get *away*." And Opal, longing, aching, lamenting, went.

A week or two later, Opal and May climbed the hill home together after helping Mabel Maude sort through Jimmy's belongings and box them up for the Goodwill. May, wonderful daughter that she was, offered to get them both a lemonade and meet her mother in the summer house. Opal entered her back garden through the gate at the side of the house and began crossing the lawn, when she was stopped in her tracks by the smell of cigarette smoke, which seemed to be coming from the summer house. Perplexed, Opal approached. When her eyes met her daughter's, Pearl lifted the cigarette to her lips. "Hello, Mother," she said.

The entire world, including her body, seemed that much heavier for Opal to carry around these days. Now that he had retired, Mac was at home *all of the time* except on the blessed days he played golf or went fishing. He helped her in the garden a little, and read copiously, but still there wasn't enough for him to do, and his nitpicking was driving her crazy. Her territory had been invaded, and they fought constantly.

"There were few enough complaints before about how I ran the house," she said.

"I hadn't the time to notice what was going on," he said.

"Well, I wish you would go and play some more golf."

"Wish away."

There was a litany of her offences that she endured listening to at least once a month. Every time the bill from the Hudson's Bay arrived, Mac had something to say about her stupid extravagances or her extravagant stupidity. Her driving was another topic: Mac believed women were too stupid to drive, and it was better for everyone concerned if they didn't. But Opal liked driving, and until Mac had retired and started hogging the car, she had gone out nearly every day shopping or visiting. But it seemed Mac found there was something offensive about his wife's getting into *his* car and pulling out of *his* driveway and driving away, leaving him home alone, poor man, abandoned and carless. Why did she have to go out anyway? he complained. He decided he would drive her everywhere, but then he complained about that, and when he came to pick her up, often well past the agreed-upon time, it was terribly embarrassing, because he would lay so long and hard on the horn until she appeared. The experiences became so humiliating that she stopped wanting to go anywhere at all except places they were going together. Her licence expired and she didn't renew it. She would just stay home.

Of her two daughters, it was no surprise that it was Pearl who almost never wrote or called. It was understandable, to a point: now Pearl had children to look after, and with her and Tom's recent move to the coast, no doubt finding the time was a bit of a challenge. But after all they had done for her, surely Pearl could make a small effort. If, as Pearl said, telephone calls were too expensive, then a short note would be better than no letter at all. Opal wanted to hear about her granddaughters! On this point she and Mac agreed: the only time Pearl could be sure to write was if they had written first suggesting they come for a visit, and then they were assured an answer by return post, trying, though thankfully not always succeeding, to nip the suggestion in the bud and dissuade them. Or if she wanted money. Why she should still need money when she was well over thirty years old and married to a doctor was a good question, but there it was. "She doesn't like us," Opal lamented. "Our daughter doesn't want us within five hundred miles of her."

"Tell me something I don't know," said Mac.

May, now living in Seattle with Fred, was much better. She at least responded, often at length, and she always answered questions. She and her father, especially, had a thriving correspondence. Since May had gone to take library science in Edmonton, she and Mac had great discussions by letter about books. Admittedly there had been rocky times right after May married Fred, when they had refused to visit her and made a point of staying north of the border on their few trips west. But it was better now.

There had been more than a decade between their daughters' weddings. Pearl had married Tom Mayfield of Banff in January 1941, in Montreal, where he was finishing his internship. For some reason Pearl had not wanted to wait until summer, or even spring, when travelling would have been easier for both the Mayfields and the Macaulays. But maybe that was why. Pearl used some vague excuse about the war, and then everyone was expected to dance to her tune. Even Mrs. Clive Mayfield, Tom's mother, who struck Opal as a woman who would prefer to be playing the fiddle. It would be interesting to see how those two would get along in the years ahead. They started their married life in Banff, but then Tom had joined the RCAF and they moved to Regina for his training. It was there that the first grandchild for both families, Ruby, was born.

When Tom heard that he would be going overseas to Topcliffe, England, Pearl got the idea in her head that she and little Ruby would move in with Opal and Mac until his return, and Pearl pushed and pushed against all objections until she got her way. They had room: May was still away at university in Edmonton. Didn't they want her, their first-born, there? Didn't they miss her, after all her years away? How could they pass up the opportunity to spend virtually unlimited time with their first and perhaps only grandchild? Opal and Mac had succumbed.

Well, that had been a disaster, hadn't it? While Opal tended to little Ruby, Pearl had stayed in bed every day until the postman came, and if he didn't have a letter from Tom to deliver, there was *h-e-l-l* to pay for everyone else, little Ruby included, for the rest of the day. Pearl spent hours every evening writing Tom letters, which were often accompanied by angry tears. Opal, who had had misgivings about the plan from the word go, finally told Pearl that she had already done her child-rearing years in spades, helping her own mother with her siblings in Winnipeg and then raising her own two. Pearl called her selfish and she called Pearl selfish and things deteriorated from there. The arrangement hadn't lasted six months.

Pearl had packed up Ruby and caught the train to Quebec, where mother and child stayed in rental accommodations until Tom's return. Relatives on both sides lost out. And Pearl hadn't even said thank-you—not for the months of help and support, not for the ride to the train station and the money with which she paid for her ticket, for heaven's sake! In fact, Pearl had barely said goodbye, though she did kiss her father on the cheek. Opal heaved a great sigh. Somehow she had managed to get on with *him*, while it was she, Opal, who had done all the work. Life, life was unfair. Unjust. At least little Ruby seemed sad to say goodbye to them, her sweet little face framed with white fur crumpling with tears, her small hands in their little white gloves, holding Opal's own.

Now Pearl and Tom were living on the west coast, and had bought a house and property of their own—with help from them for the down payment, of course.

And then there was that whole mess May got herself into. May had finished university and was back living at home and working at the public library downtown, and Opal had thought they were in for some calm waters. But that summer Fred, a Scot from Dundee, had been hired as the church organist and choir leader. He was immediately a great hit with everyone, the Macaulays included. He was affable, and gifted as a musician and teacher.

The Macaulays had him over for dinner often, and Mac, Opal and May had all enjoyed his company. But when it became apparent that he was turning his attentions specifically towards May, that was a different kettle of fish. How dare he, a man twenty years her senior? He had no business courting a young girl like that. Opal felt he had betrayed their hospitality, and their trust. She took him aside politely to suggest that it was not appropriate, that he was taking advantage of a young girl's naïveté. But nothing Opal said dissuaded him. In fact, her objections seemed to make him more, not less, resolved, and May, completely lacking experience when it came to matters of the heart, was easy prey. She was moonstruck. And giddy. And silly as Opal had never before seen her. She was more like Lillie than like herself. Never mind that she was almost thirty; she was completely innocent and susceptible to his machinations.

The situation only got worse when it was revealed that Fred was in fact a married man! He already *had* a wife! How dare he set his sights on May?! Opal was faint with outrage. Fred would not be invited to their home again, but she had felt only temporary victory because now the whole wretched affair was continuing in secret. Whenever May left the house, Opal suspected she was going to meet him, but what could she say? And she couldn't forbid May from singing in the church choir. The whole business was deeply humiliating for Opal, and she could not hold her head up. She almost stopped going to church.

The day came that Fred hand-delivered a note in which he insisted upon seeing them the following day, either in their home or at a restaurant. She was not about to discuss anything with that man in a public place, so what could she do? She told Mac she doubted she could stay in the same room with him, but Mac said they had better get it over with and hear the man out. All right, said Opal. But she would not offer him tea.

Fred said right out that his intention was to marry May. He said that he had asked her and that she had accepted.

"Well, this is the first we've heard of it," snapped Opal.

Fred said nothing.

"And what does your wife have to say about it?" asked Opal.

"Agnes is my wife in name only," said Fred.

"But a wife nonetheless." Well, what had happened to his marriage? Opal wanted to know. And where exactly was his current wife?

He had parted ways with Agnes York years before, he said, well before he had come to Canada, because Agnes had told him flat out that she had—and he quoted—"no inclination whatsoever towards the pioneering life," and wanted to stay where she was, in Dundee. (Pioneering life indeed, thought Opal. You would think they were a bunch of savages.) She was terrified, Fred said, with an attempt at levity, of the Indians. So he had set sail alone. He said that he and she were too young when he married. They did not know their own minds. Which was no longer the case with him. He knew exactly what he wanted, and when, and whom, and that whom was their daughter May.

He might as well tell them now, he added, that he had been offered and had accepted a teaching job at a college near Seattle, a tenured position, and that he and May would be moving there in September, soon after they were married. They would marry this coming summer.

Now Opal had heard enough, more than enough to confirm her worst suspicions. She stood purposefully, expecting Mac to usher Fred to the front door. She had her parting words prepared: he was never to darken their doorstep again. He was never to telephone this house again. Never mind what May wanted. But Mac let Opal down. "Come upstairs," he motioned to Fred. And the two of them went up to Mac's study, where, she was sure, Mac got out the bottle of Scotch he had hidden there and thought she knew nothing about. Ha. Dollars to doughnuts she would be able to smell the liquor on them when they came back. Before long she heard them up there, sharing a laugh like brothers while she, down here, and alone, was on her third hanky. May was nowhere in sight. When Opal heard the men descending the stairs, she fled to the summer house. There, she wept some more.

This marriage couldn't possibly be what God had in mind for May. Her future had been unfolding nicely. What purpose could it possibly serve to quit a good job and leave now? And leave not only Calgary but her whole country? What use would her education be down there?

"What about children?" she asked May, when she finally caught up with her and they shared a cup of tea. "Twenty years' difference in age, dear."

"We don't want children," said May, "and if we did, so what? It wouldn't be the first time in history someone had an old father, would it?" There was fight in May's voice. Just look what that man had done to her. Where had Opal's pleasant, agreeable daughter gone?

For the first time in her life, May had spoken back to her mother. Was not always willing to help. Was not always soft-hearted and kind. It wasn't the university or the job that had done this to her—it was that man. What, oh, what was Opal to do? May could without doubt see what she was doing to her mother, the pain she was causing her, and yet she had hardened her heart against the very person who loved her best in this world, and she would not budge in her conviction that she would marry this man, and marry him soon.

It was more than a month before Opal could bring herself to tell her family in Winnipeg about the whole mess, and that was only when May announced that she wanted the wedding to take place there, and she would not listen to alternatives that would have enabled Opal to conceal the details. No one in Winnipeg took Opal's side either; no one would fight alongside her for what was right. Only her mother objected, and only mildly. "In the end, there's not much you can do about it, is there?" Georgie said. Opal's sister Lillie went on about how love was where you found it, and what fun they were going to have planning the wedding. Even Pearl found the time to write and offer her two cents' worth, which was to say that at her age May should surely be allowed to make up her own mind.

Well, if no one else cared, said Opal to herself, she would soldier on alone. She would fight tooth and nail. But then one day when she had gone into May's room—to check on the maid's progress—she found a letter hidden between the mattress and the box springs. She sat down on May's bed and read it, and realized she would not win this fight.

Monday, March 5, 1951
My darling bud of May,

There has never been any doubt in my mind, sweetheart, regarding you and me. That was just as sure as the day follows the night. We both knew it long before we admitted it to each other, didn't we, lass? And I don't feel that there is anything wrong at all about it. Had I been living with my wife, yes! But the end of my marriage to Agnes happened long before I met and fell in love with you. Dearest, it is so easy for people who have never had this sort of love to try and live our lives for us. But they can't. And they can't know what we are feeling.

I don't think your parents have been very fair to either of us, dearest. They both know me well, and I see no reason for them taking their present attitude. Your Ma has certainly done her level best to ruin my reputation, I must say, and I certainly resent it. However, I have an idea that she will be the one to suffer in the end. Insofar as we are concerned, darling, there isn't anything I want from them anyway, except their regard . . . and their bonnie daughter. And I'll have both, one of these days. Though the first will be much harder to get from "Ma" than from "Pa."

Ah, my Mayflower. Now give me that beautiful mouth again, darling. You are so very lovely.

Yours always,
Fred

Fred Haig finally obtained his divorce in the United States, though Opal had serious doubts as to its authenticity and legitimacy. But in the end, there was nothing for them to do but go. She left a letter saying as much on May's bed.

May 28, 1952
Dear May,

Your father and I will be at your wedding. But you must not think, dear, that we have given our consent or agreed to go because we are any more reconciled to the situation, or that we feel happy at all about it. Rather, it is because of our great love for you. If you want us to be there, we want to go, and if you have your heart set on Winnipeg, then so be it.

I hope you will understand my feelings, and realize that I mention the causes of my concern only because I love you so much. I hope now that, as you say, "we can close the subject entirely."

Love and Kisses, Mother

Lillie helped May get ready for her wedding day. Lillie and Malcolm held a big dinner for May and Fred the night before the wedding, at their big posh house. No doubt they all had drinks celebrating the impending wedding, and laughed, and had a jolly old time saying, What would Opal think! It wasn't right. Where was the bride's mother in all this? In a hotel room with her cranky husband who wanted to be at the party instead of with her, that's where.

So Opal went to her daughter's wedding in the end, but she wore her second-best dress and would not shake hands with her new son-in-law in the minister's study.

Opal

Opal and Mac arrived in White Rock on a Wednesday afternoon in May after their visit with May and Fred down in Seattle. The train trip across the border had been pleasant enough, and uneventful. It was a nice surprise to see all of Pearl's family, excepting Tom, gathered at the station to meet them before taking them to the town of Beresford, where Tom and Pearl lived. They had gone to a restaurant for lunch, but both the food and the service were poor; Mac would describe it later as about as crummy a meal as he had ever experienced. Unfortunately, the situation would turn out to be the same at the Beresford Hotel, where Pearl had arranged for them to stay.

The visits they had every day with Pearl and her family were pretty nice, though Pearl was often dreadfully late picking them up at the hotel. The household was somewhat hectic and sometimes chaotic. The eldest, Ruby, was nowhere to be seen much of the time, squirrelled away with a book; the second, Laurel, was rather unruly and disobedient—she had painted the wall of her room with her watercolours while they were there—but Opal put that down to attention-seeking, and being a little jealous of the attention the two younger girls necessarily got from their mother. But they were much smaller children, three and four, and Amethyst had both allergies and asthma, and needed more attention. Actually, Pearl seemed to favour Amethyst above all the children, so it wasn't all fabrication on Laurel's part. Little Vivien, the youngest, seemed often to get lost in the shuffle, and had glommed right on to her grandmother as though she were a lifebuoy. Opal always found her hanging around nearby, asking to climb up in her lap, putting her little hands on Opal's face, lifting the netting of her hat off her face, planting wet kisses wherever she could find space. Opal liked the child. Together they brushed their hair and got ready for bed, and more than once Vivien fell asleep curled up against her.

Pearl and Tom's house was looking much better than it had during last year's visit. It had a new roof, and Pearl had hired a neighbour man to put in some gardens, which looked quite nice—a triangular pansy bed near the front door, and a rose arbour through the middle of the front lawn left to right, with a cherry tree on either end. Opal and Mac escaped the house and went for a bit of a stroll after supper one evening when the rain let up—temporarily, of course—and they had discovered raspberry canes, and a thicket of blackberries that would soon be in bloom. The family seemed right at home. The rose arbour looked especially nice from the living room and bedrooms. Improvements were still under way. Tom spent one Sunday digging a large hole for what he said would be a lily pond. He mixed cement in a wheelbarrow, and worked away until past dark, and Pearl was cross with him for being late for dinner.

On the Saturday, the day of their departure, Pearl drove them into Vancouver, taking Ruby to her piano lesson and Laurel to a ballet lesson. The two youngsters had been dropped off at a babysitter's, and how they had cried and carried on, saying goodbye to Gramma and Grampop! They had hung off her legs, hopped up and down—what a scene! Opal herself had found it hard not to join them with her own tears.

After the girls' lessons, they had a light lunch on the sixth floor of the Hudson's Bay before Pearl drove them to the CPR station, where she had let them out at the front doors and left them to fend for themselves with their luggage. Their train didn't depart for another four hours, so they had plenty of time. They could have had one more hour of visiting, but Pearl was clearly glad to be seeing the backs of them. "We've been visiting for a *week*," she exclaimed, as though she'd survived an ordeal. Not only that, she added, but she really had to get back to get Tom's supper on.

That afternoon, Opal had finished planting her glads, and now she surveyed the patted earth outside the dining room window with satisfaction. The hardest work was done; she could simply wait until she saw green shoots poke through the earth, as the plants began their work making the tall, strong stalks. When she held the bulbs in her hands each spring, she was amazed and awed each time at God's handiwork. How could such an unremarkable-looking brown, wrinkly, rootlike thing produce such spectacular flowers?!

Now she had changed out of her gardening clothes and straightened up the bedroom. She could smell supper cooking in the kitchen. She'd asked Audrey, their new girl, to have their meal ready for six. Maybe she was going to work out after all. Now that girls no longer lived with the people they worked for, Opal had found them less reliable, more likely to be late arriving and doing their work, though never late when departing. Audrey would be changing into her street shoes and slipping out the back door at the earliest possible moment.

Right before dinner, the florist delivered Opal a lovely rose corsage, a Mother's Day gift from May. How happy its arrival had made her! She would ask Mac to help her pin it on when he came down for dinner. What a perfume it had! She would wear it to church in the morning. What a fine daughter May was! She never missed an important date, and she never failed to write or telephone every week. Thank goodness for one daughter with a heart and a conscience. Opal's mouth tightened into a straight line. She hadn't heard from Pearl. Or the granddaughters. In fact, there hadn't been a word from any of them for ages, not for Mac's birthday last month or Mother's Day now. What was the matter with them?

This morning Audrey had helped Opal carry the bulbs up from the basement, and before he left for an afternoon golf game Mac had helped her prepare the soil, turning it over with a gardening fork. It would be a while before she saw signs of growth: the weather all week had been chilly, and looked to continue that way for a while yet. This morning, before she had gone outside, there had been rain, and then as she finished and was coming back in the house, some snowflakes had started falling. In May! Well, you never knew in this climate. Now, though, as she turned to go into the dining room for dinner, she saw that the sky was clear and there were stars coming out.

Opal took her place at the table and waited for Mac. She was hungry. Her hands fidgeted in her lap. The telephone hadn't rung once today. Well, perhaps tomorrow. After supper, and a cup of tea in the living room with Mac, Opal drew the drapes across the living room windows, across the stars and the deep blue sky, and went up to bed.

Their next trip to Beresford was no better than the last, except that the children were older. It rained the whole time and the sky was so dark and gloomy that the atmosphere both inside and out was truly oppressive. Pearl complained endlessly about her lot, and about Tom and all that he was not doing that Pearl thought he should be doing. Tom was uncommunicative. Tom shirked his responsibilities. Every day, the wife of Tom's medical partner went off in her pickup truck to spend the afternoon in the beer parlour (how sordid! thought Opal). The four girls sulked and wailed and fought and clamoured for attention Pearl did not give them, until Opal felt she couldn't hold her tongue one minute longer, though she had.

At home, Mac spent much of his time fishing, or golfing, or reading up in his study, while Opal puttered about below. Mac liked spending time alone more than she did. But they did go out together. Just last Tuesday they had gone to the Jubilee Auditorium to see the National Ballet, and the performance was on the whole pretty good, Opal had thought, especially the part called "Offenbach in the Underworld." But Mac had not cared much for the second part, which featured five male dancers wearing ballet tights. If she and Mac hadn't been in the middle of the row, he might have got up and left. In the car on the way home, Mac had ranted about the performance and how he did not get much of a kick out of seeing men cavorting around in tights. Indeed, he said, once or twice he had felt like bursting out laughing. Thank goodness, thought Opal, that he hadn't.

Well, Mac was in better humour overall these days, why she could not say, but as a result so was she. He hadn't flown into a rage since who knew when, and he got more upset about golf scores than about anything else. There were good things about getting older, though not many, as far as Opal could tell. She disliked the weight she had gained; she disliked how much more difficult it was for her to get around, even to go up and down the stairs. When the last girl had quit on them, Mac had suggested doing without, but she had put the kibosh on that in a hurry.

Both she and Mac had felt pretty tired after their Christmas vacation in Beresford. Between the two of them they must have washed and dried a thousand dishes. Every time they turned around there were more to do, stacked up by the sink. Their dishwashing machine was on the blink, Pearl said, and the repairman hadn't shown up. Pearl was still adding to her long list of Tom's failings, the most recent entry being that he was lazy. It did not seem so to Opal. Tom appeared to be busy as could be, coming and going from the hospital and going out on calls in the middle of the night in addition to his office hours, but Pearl did not see it that way. Any word Opal or Mac might murmur in Tom's defence was construed by Pearl as a word against her. "You always take his side," Pearl would have objected had Opal said a word, and yet another topic would be closed and another source of tension added to the growing heap.

Pearl never seemed to respond to any of the little affectionate advances Tom made, which didn't help matters, and the goings-on of the children, who seemed particularly unruly—as if Pearl was letting them run wild and waiting for him to take charge in the discipline department while he clearly felt otherwise—obviously got on Tom's nerves. The children were not even required to remain at the table from the time they sat down until they finished their meals. Tom would get fed up and go off to the living room and play the piano for an hour, off in his own little world, as if that was the only peace and enjoyment he could find in his own home.

Opal would have to write a note to May and then include it with the letter Mac had already written, which was lying on the sideboard. He communicated with May more often than she did; their relationship seemed to be the best of them all.

June 1960
Dear May,

Well, the papers this last week have been swamped with advertisements of "Father's Day." Thank goodness I warned Pearl and you off this Father's Day business years ago, so that I will not have to look forward to thanking either

Pearl or you for a Power Mower or a high-powered rifle.

I have omitted in my last two or three letters mentioning Doctor Zhivago. *I struggle with it every night for half an hour or so after I go to bed. Possibly I have no true literary taste, but where this book gets its reputation is beyond me. Really I find it very boring but I soldier on in the hope that it may improve. I am two-thirds of the way through now.*

I have now finished the story of Hannibal. What a general! Greater even than Napoleon, I believe. I enjoyed not only the reading of it but also translating the copious notes in Latin and Greek by Livy and Polybius respectively. Over the course of my reading I have developed a great interest in Hannibal. He was such a marvellous man and yet ended his life in frustration.

Our garden is looking quite nice now. However, the gardener is slipshod in his work and so the garden does not have the well-clipped look it should have. (One certainly has to be content with very little nowadays from workmen and cleaning women. I wonder what it will be like twenty-five years from now.) The gardener put the pansies and sweet peas in last week. Your mother's glads are appearing and we have a few leaves on the trees. Everything is behind, though, as the weather has been rather cool much of the time recently.

I took a great deal of interest in the Democratic and Republican conventions, as I think did most Canadians. The last-minute alliances between Kennedy and Johnson for the Democrats and Nixon and Rockefeller for the Republicans left most Canadians like myself somewhat mystified.

Love,

Dad

Eventually, Opal broke down and wrote to Pearl asking her please to make clear whether she wanted them to go to her house for Christmas or not. She explained as nicely as she could that they needed to do some planning, so they needed to know. To be on the safe side Mac had gone down to make the reservations on the train, in case Pearl answered in the affirmative. Even so, he could not get them the dates they wanted; he had to take a bedroom leaving on the Thursday before Christmas, which Opal was afraid Pearl would not like, because after the time they had stayed a week, Pearl never wanted to be bothered with them more than two days before Christmas and two days after. Pearl might think Thursday was too soon for them to arrive, and tell them they would be in her way.

While they waited for a response, Opal fretted. She tried to focus on making her annual list of ingredients for her Christmas baking, but she couldn't concentrate and kept misplacing the list and then having to start over. What if Pearl said no again? What then? What would her family in Winnipeg think if they weren't with their grandchildren for Christmas? Pearl and May had always been in Winnipeg with their grandparents for

Christmas. Watching as they opened their parcels. The uncertainty was breaking Opal's heart. Each day, she fretted until the mailman came, empty-handed. Here it was, almost December. They simply had to get an answer from her pretty soon. She wanted Mac to telephone, but he wouldn't. "That would be the wrong thing to do," he said. "And you may have noticed that we are always doing the wrong thing as far as Pearl is concerned."

"Pooh," Opal had retorted.

On December 1, they received Pearl's letter. Pearl did not want them to come. So that was that. Opal felt let down, and she knew that Mac did too, though he would never admit it. They would be alone for Christmas, then, here in Calgary. Opal wailed that Pearl hadn't even given any reasons, any explanation at all. She hadn't sounded sad or sorry for one second.

"Why should that surprise you?" said Mac.

"But why doesn't she tell us what is the matter?"

"When has Pearl ever expressed any regard for our feelings? Being secretive is her modus operandi. You can never pry anything out of her unless she wants you to."

Opal tried to talk Mac into going out to the coast anyway. They could stay at the Beresford Hotel and keep out from underfoot at Pearl's. Mac flatly refused. He said he could not see where that would get them except into more hot water. He said she should go out alone. But she didn't want to. "We should go together," she said. Mac repeated that he would not butt in where he was not wanted. "Case closed," he said.

Opal sat for hours every day on the green fibreglass chair outside Mac's hospital room, steadily knitting her way through ball after ball of coral-coloured mohair wool. In the bottom of her knitting bag she had Mac's book in case he should ask for it, *The Rise and Fall of the Roman Empire*, which he had ordered as an early birthday present to himself. But she would not go into his room.

Once she finished this sleeve and sewed the pieces together and blocked the sweater and then sewed on the flat mother-of-pearl buttons, she would have knit each of her granddaughters a new cardigan. This coral one was for the youngest, Vivien. Opal concentrated on what she was doing, increase, decrease, though given the number of sweaters she had knit in her life, she could have almost done it blind.

Inside the hospital room, Mac, conscious and aware that he was likely dying from this, his second heart attack, lay unmoving, his hands at his sides on top of the covers. He did not read. He did not eat or drink. His glasses lay folded on the bedside table. He did not ask for Opal, or for Pearl or May. He did not ask for a thing. And then, one week before his eighty-second birthday, he died, with the door of his hospital room firmly shut between him and his wife, and that's the way their life together ended, with him on the inside and her on the outside, knitting.

Shortly after his death, Opal learned that Mac had made all legal arrangements long before. He had not said anything about them to her, he had not involved her in any of the decisions, and the instructions came as a terrible surprise. He had instructed his executor, a trust company, to undertake the selling of the house and car as soon after his death as possible. It would be too much for a woman alone to handle, he noted, and he had wanted, according to the man from the trust company, to simplify matters for her.

Simplify? Simplify? How did robbing her of her home simplify anything? Opal saw his actions as deliberate cruelty, a final affirmation of what she had always suspected: that he did not love her, nor even like her, and this—this was his *coup de grâce.* This house was *hers.* She had wanted to live here for the rest of her life. How dare he? How could he? How she had revelled in doing all that she had been unable to do before, in that other house. She had decorated the house completely, she had grown all the flowers in its gardens. This house was *home,* and she loved it with all her heart.

But there was no time to adjust to anything. Now, with the world shifted greatly beneath her, and long before she was ready to face further change, Opal faced the For Sale sign in the middle of the lawn. Trust company. Who could trust them? At night she cried in fear and loneliness, and during the day, if the agent brought people by, she hid in the summer house or downstairs in the cold room. She could barely make a cup of tea without losing track of what she was doing, and when the house sold and the date of her eviction neared, she became frantic with worry yet was unable to string two thoughts together to help herself. Pain and anger sloshed weakly around inside her as she stood empty and alone in her bedroom looking out, her eyes fixed on her large, unkempt flower beds, remembering how they used to be, the glads tall and beautiful, packed with their prizewinning blooms. This year she hadn't even got the bulbs in; here it was July and they were still wrapped in paper in the basement.

Opal sat in her new apartment's living room and looked out the window at the traffic on Seventeenth Avenue. Soon it would be Christmas, and she would be spending it alone for the first time. Last year at this time she was baking cookies and shopping for presents. Mac was at home. And now? Who would spend Christmas with her? Who would take her in? She couldn't go back to Winnipeg. Her sister Lillie had her hands full with her socialite's life and their poor loony brother Melville, and Lillie couldn't have, or wouldn't want, a gloomy widow hanging around. Her brothers Reggie, Farley, Jimmy—all of them were dead; her sister Pearly K was dead. Her daughter Pearl didn't want her, had never wanted her, and neither did May's husband. She would have to get through Christmas somehow.

In February, as a snowstorm raged outside, Opal put aside her pride and called Pearl. She could hear the vacuum going in the background. Pearl hated vacuuming. "I was wondering," Opal said. "Do you think—" She hesitated. "Do you think I could try coming to live with you for a little while? I could help with the children."

After a long pause, Pearl said, "You have a nice new apartment, Mother. Which I helped you find, you may remember. You can't just leave it."

"It's a very nice apartment, Pearl, it really is, but I'm so terribly lonely these days. I don't see anyone. Pearl?" Opal's right hand fidgeted with a digestive cracker and a small pile of crumbs beside it.

Pearl heaved a martyr's heavy sigh into the phone, a sigh that said she could certainly live without such attempts at emotional manipulation. A sigh that also said how could you say no to such a request from your own mother? "On a trial basis then, Mother," Pearl finally said. And Opal hung up the telephone both relieved and sad, and dabbed her tearful eyes with her handkerchief, one of the handkerchiefs she had stitched so many years ago for her trousseau.

Opal emerged from her bedroom at Pearl's and walked slowly along the hardwood hall towards the steps that led down into the living room, where Pearl had just finished watering her African violets. Opal could see Amy and Vivien, eight and seven, standing behind the glass door of the playroom, watching. Now Pearl was turning the plants in the indirect sunlight so that the lay of their leaves would be uniform. "Would you like a little drink?" Opal heard her ask the violets kindly. "It will help you grow. Is that better?" Amy and Vivien knocked on the glass and smiled and waved at their grandmother. Their mother looked up, first at them, then at her mother, and absorbed what she was seeing.

"Mother!" she said sharply. "Look what you're doing!"

Opal stopped, looked around her, looked at the floor, saw the puddle between her feet.

"I'm standing in some water," she said with hesitation in her voice. "Someone's spilled a little water. I can get a cloth . . ."

Pearl stood up like an ogress and moved aggressively towards her mother. Opal shrank back. Amy and Vivien turned away. Poor Gramma. She had been there only a week and already she was driving their mother around the bend. "Oh for heaven's sake, Mother, it's *urine*," Pearl said now. "I can't spend my days mopping up after you. You're not a *child*, Mother! Oh, *damn it all* anyway!" And her voice rose in its familiar martyr's wail.

"Oh my," said Opal, embarrassed, backing away. "Oh my goodness." As quickly as she could, she turned into her room and shut the door behind her.

At the nursing home Pearl found for her in White Rock, Opal stayed in bed. Sorrow and confusion were etched deeper and deeper in her face, while her knitting lay untouched on her bedside table. During one visit Pearl left the room to talk to the nurse, and Opal, trying to find something to say to the little girls, smiled wanly at Amy and Vivien and said, "Would you like to see my scar? From my operation?" The children exchanged glances. What operation? It was rude to say nothing. It would be rude to say no, even though something about this was not right. Confused, Vivien said, "Okay." Opal laboured to hike her hospital gown up past her waist. The children saw her big soft white thighs, the funny thick white underwear. "Right here," said Opal. Then Pearl walked in. "*Stop* that, Mother!" she ordered. She pushed Amy and Vivien aside and yanked up the bedding. "Pull down your nightdress! Hell's *bells*, Mother, what is *wrong* with you?!"

Opal took her purse from her bedside table, checked the wad of cash in the bottom of her knitting bag, put on her slip and her navy blue dress with the tiny white polka dots, and even managed her girdle and stockings. No one commented when she walked out the front door, and no one noticed when she got into the cab that was waiting for somebody else. "To the CPR station," she said with authority, the way Mac would have said it, and in less than an hour she had used her lifetime CPR pass and boarded a train to Calgary. She smiled as the train took her home: everything had lined up. At the Calgary station she caught another cab, and on the way to her apartment Opal asked the driver to stop at a grocery store and go in and buy her two quarts of vanilla ice cream. A week later, the home care nurse found Opal dead, lying on her rose-coloured jacquard chesterfield beneath the front room window and nestled in a pale green satin duvet, a dessert bowl and spoon on the otherwise empty table beside her.

PEARL

The biggest pleasure of Pearl Macaulay's life so far had been, without question, leaving home for the first time, setting off on the university train into the great unknown, off to Montreal to study English Literature and Art History, off to the best university in the country, according to her father. Adieu! she had called out the window, and smiled broadly at her parents. The look of astonishment on her mother's face still made her smile. Ha! She had no idea her daughter could look so happy, did she? How little she knew her. And Pearl *was* happy. Every year at this time. Leaving her mother's stupid badgering, her father's sudden explosions of anger, her placid and boring goody two-shoes little sister. Never mind all that. She was setting out on an adventure. She was setting out on her *life* and she was leaving all that had hobbled her behind.

Now, returning, she felt that same delicious sense of release. But it was a much more mature approach now, she was sure, and refined. She looked forward to her studies, to the stacks of new books to read, to seeing the girlfriends she had made, Marion and Esther. She liked belonging to Kappa Alpha Theta with them, and playing badminton, and attending the elegant parties and dances to which she wore her evening gowns and gloves and her deep red velvet opera cape with the ermine collar and was asked to dance, sometimes by tall fellows with red hair. She smiled. There was nothing she didn't like about life at McGill. Nothing. She wondered if Manny with the red hair would be back. He had hoped to return, he said, but there had been some doubt and they hadn't communicated further. What a waltz they had had. She could still feel his hand on her back.

Pearl took up her book, glanced at her wristwatch and began to read. She was reading a forbidden book, her current favourite: D.H. Lawrence's *Sons and Lovers.* This would be her third time through, and it wasn't on any of her university reading lists. But so what? Live a little, she told herself. What fun was there in doing what you were told all the time?

After reading for an hour, she closed the book, keeping her fingers inside against the words and closing the covers so the book squeezed her fingertips. Her body was awake and aching. No wonder Lawrence had been censored. He was banned from the house by her parents, too. She snickered. This summer, thinking to enlighten them, or at least startle them into an awareness of the real world, she had left the book in the summer house. It was gone when she returned the next day, and she had had to retrieve it from the kindling bin where one of them had tossed it. A smile played on her lips. They had probably used tongs. Ha! What prudes her parents were! She gave a small snort of contempt, and the woman across from her raised her head from her magazine. Pearl met her pale blue eyes, blinked, and turned her head to the window. They were so rigid, her parents, both of them. And how laughable her mother was, the way she "stuck to her guns" even when doing so flew in the face of logic. She was pathetic, really. And her father—well, she would always adore him, but not his atrocious temper. When he became angry, it was like a huge, sudden thunderclap that made everything around it shake. And cry.

She lay back and closed her eyes. Free! She was free of all that for the next three and a half months.

Aunt Pearly K and Grandpa King were waiting for Pearl at the Winnipeg station—she identified her aunt at once by the wide-striped blouse she was wearing—Aunt Pearly K loved stripes—and she gave them both a smile and a wave out the train window. She would be staying overnight, resuming her trip to Montreal tomorrow. Her aunt and grandfather had come directly from the horse races, they explained as they embraced her, and she could smell the manure and the beer. Good thing Mother isn't here! she thought. Ha! They said they had been concerned about being late and so hadn't stopped at the hardware store to pick up Melville, which wouldn't make him happy and so, said Aunt Pearly K, there would be hell to pay when they got home. "Oh well," she said with a grin at her niece. In her humble opinion Melville always got what he wanted, so he deserved to learn better.

Pearl enjoyed the time with the Kings. She always did. She always thought of them fondly, even Uncle Melville, who was so strange the way he spoke with a giggle and normally wouldn't look at you but if he did it was with this long, pale, unnerving look as though he were looking at a part of you that you didn't know existed.

She always felt somehow nicer after spending time with them all, though the feeling never lasted. They loved each other, this family, and they loved her, and there was something clean and uncomplicated about their kind of love. What was the matter with her own family? Why did they get her in such knots and make her so unhappy? Why did they make her so mad? Well, she wouldn't have to think about any of that for a while. Thank heavens. And thank heavens for her Winnipeg relatives, who didn't criticize her every minute of the day or jump out of nowhere to attack her. Hallelujah!

The train pulled out of the Winnipeg station and Pearl leaned back. Maybe she wouldn't go home for Christmas. Maybe one of her girlfriends would invite her for the holidays. She could go to Knowlton with Marion. Imagine the looks on her parents' faces when they heard she wasn't coming home. Ha! It would serve them right. Give them pause to reflect on how they treated her. But she'd have to go back eventually. Why was nothing ever perfect? Nothing. There was something wrong with everything. She tilted her seat back as far as it would go and relaxed her body, and thought about Lawrence, and allowed the train to sway her back and forth.

Pearl was taken completely by surprise when Tom Mayfield proposed to her. They hadn't been dating very long, and a wedding engagement was the furthest thing from her mind. She barely knew him, in fact. They'd played badminton a few times. Before that, she had just seen him, along with his younger brother,

William, in the McGill car of the university train as they travelled across the country. She had never spoken to them, though she knew they were from Banff. Their father was a doctor and worked, as her father did, for the CPR. Their aunt attended the same church in Calgary as her parents. That's about all she knew about the Mayfields until October, when Eleanor, Tom's mother, had started pushing Tom towards her. Eleanor Mayfield's little note was Pearl's first experience with her future mother-in-law—such a pretty note, suggesting that she and Tom might play a game of badminton and get to know each other. And they had. Why not? He was not as good a player as she, and she'd let him win so that his fragile male ego wouldn't suffer too much. Ha! And so that he might ask her out again. Which he did. He was very quiet, and shy, and she felt responsible for carrying the conversation and asking him twenty times more questions than he asked her. But he seemed to like her well enough. They played badminton again, and then they settled into a kind of routine, getting together on weekends and occasionally taking in a show. They sat together part of the way on the trip home and back at Christmas. They went to a musical, then a dance. Then another.

In the spring of 1940, Tom's parents had come for a visit—they were en route to England and their ship would sail from Montreal. Pearl hadn't expected to see Tom that weekend, which was just as well; she was sick in bed with a bad cold and could barely think straight. She wasn't in the mood for visiting, let alone romance. When she could think about anything at all, she thought about the badminton tournament she was missing, and the Chaucer exam she was going to fail on Monday if she couldn't study. Her intermittent sleep was filled with Middle

English phrases she couldn't remember and badminton shots she missed.

She roused herself and came down to the common room in her housecoat to meet Tom. She wondered why that darn tic on his face was going so strongly, why his voice was so low and tremulous, why he had so much trouble meeting her eyes with his. Then all was revealed, as he forged ahead with his proposal of marriage. Astounded, she was able to blurt out "Yes," and to offer some semblance of grace and appreciation in spite of her runny nose and red eyes. At least she had combed her hair. It, anyway, was presentable.

"You'd better not kiss me," she said. "I don't want to give you this cold." So they shook hands instead. Both hands.

Jewellery had never been high on Pearl's list of desires, but still, wasn't there supposed to be a ring? Tactfully, she hoped, she asked after an engagement ring's existence or whereabouts.

"There is one, but it isn't here," said Tom.

"Where is it?"

"Henry Birks."

"Gee, that's too bad. Well, can you tell me what it's like?"

"I don't know what it's like. I haven't seen it."

"Oh," said Pearl.

It turned out that his mother had picked out the ring herself, because, after all, she said, she and his father were paying for it. She had given Tom explicit instructions (they were written down and tucked into his breast pocket) on how the day was to unfold: propose to Pearl after lunch; take Pearl to pick up the ring at Henry Birks'; meet Mother and Dad in their suite at the hotel at four for the presentation of the ring; and then go out for dinner, the four of them, in the hotel's dining room. Pearl dressed and went along with Tom reluctantly. She did not want to meet his parents when she still felt so ill, and she did not appreciate being railroaded by someone's mother: it made her want to run in the other direction. However, she didn't want to jeopardize the engagement. You had to marry someone, and no one else had shown much interest in dating let alone marrying her. Manny her red-headed dance partner had never returned. And she and Tom liked each other well enough and got along reasonably well, and they *definitely* enjoyed kissing each other. That was, above all, the very best thing about their relationship. The touch of their hot, sweaty bodies after a game. The touch of their hot, wet hands. The hugs of defeat and of victory.

As they followed his mother's instructions to a T, Pearl was getting crankier by the minute. Ha, she thought. Is this how it's going to be? Mama this, Mama that? Today and every day? It seemed so, given the letters Eleanor wrote.

Banff, Alberta
June 28, 1940
Dearest Tom,

We arrived home yesterday and I'm still weary from our big trip. Daddy looks tired too. I will write further about our time in England, but right now there are more pressing matters.

We certainly enjoyed meeting with you and your Pearl, and having dinner with you after the presentation of the ring. Pearl seems to be a very sweet girl, and Daddy is highly pleased about your engagement too.

Darling, I have had time to think since leaving you, and if you have not already written to Mr. Macaulay formally asking for Pearl's hand, I hope you'll send an air mail off immediately, doing so. You see, Mr. Macaulay is "old country" and he seems to me to be quite a formal person. I think he would expect such a letter. As well, I think it would be nice to write a separate letter to Mrs. Macaulay on the matter. One does not marry the whole family, but there is consideration due those who have spent thousands of dollars and years of care on your girl. Please attend to both these letters at once. Don't procrastinate, dear!

And dear, you must be very definite and very prompt in letting us know the price of the bride's bouquet, and corsages for the bride's mother and for the bridesmaid, if Pearl is having one, so that we can take care of the financial end of things. Is she, dear? Since you may be in the service soon, it seems a shame to buy a new suit, so you might wear a dark suit freshly pressed, if the wedding is in the afternoon, or, better, wear tails for an evening wedding, since you have those already. That would call for white gloves, I suppose. Are you having an attendant, and if so, whom? There would be his gift and the organist's. Get right down to business re details and do not leave them until the last. *Mr. Macaulay is very businesslike and I feel he may be a little impatient of indefiniteness. Make up your mind and stick to it. Mr. Macaulay must know what to wear too, tails, or tux, or dark suit, and he'll expect you to tell him. Is anyone singing? Your cousin Charlotte, perhaps? Will you have William for best man or organist?*

Aunt Annie is quite thrilled over the wedding, and pleased about Pearl. Daddy and I are awfully pleased about Pearl too, and we hope you will make each other happy.

Daddy will enclose twelve dollars, your June allowance. Heaps of love to you both,

XXXXxxxx Mama

Pearl didn't like the ring, though she hadn't said so to anyone except Tom. In the years ahead, whenever she looked at it, she would think of Eleanor Mayfield's bossy, smiling face and hear her saying, "Because we are *paying* for it."

Then, in November, Eleanor suddenly decided that Pearl and Tom should marry early in 1941. In January, in fact. What, Pearl wondered, was the big rush? Why not wait for spring or summer, for sunshine and warmth? Well, that was easy enough to figure out after a very little bit of thought. Right after his October birthday, Eleanor Mayfield's good boy Tom had broken one of the rules at McGill, and his parents had been officially informed. Tom had taken one of the maids who worked in his residence out for coffee, and someone had seen and reported them. Ye gods! You would have thought they'd been discovered in sexual *flagrante delicto* given the uproar that ensued.

There were maids all over the place at McGill in those days, and they weren't all of them good girls, certainly. It was common knowledge that some of the maids who worked in the residences, attending to the men's housekeeping and laundry needs, went out on the sly with the men. It was rare for anyone to be caught, however, and rarer still to receive a reprimand, formal or otherwise. But Tom, who swore up and down that he had been on an innocent mission related to laundry, had been both caught and reprimanded.

Of course Pearl herself had known all about it well ahead of time, as his *fiancée*, and hadn't been concerned for a minute: the girl was homely and not bright, and whatever his interest in her, it most definitely wasn't of a sexual nature. And anyway, Pearl had that part of him cornered. Pearl figured that Eleanor Mayfield, for whom social propriety and reputation were paramount, had been thrown into a perfect tizzy by the reprimand. Eleanor had become so worried that her precious elder son was going to end up compelled to marry one of the maids instead of someone of his own station, i.e., Pearl, that she had yet again taken matters into her own hands. Without bringing the matter up as she should have with Tom's *affianced*, Eleanor decided to solve the matter by pushing the wedding plans ahead, under some invented guise of a wedding present—a honeymoon ski trip in the Laurentians. Wouldn't that be fun? Ha, thought Pearl. For whom? She did not ski.

Then Eleanor Mayfield topped it all by writing Pearl another of her sweet little notes, this time about the importance of making oneself available to one's husband, "every night." Eleanor needn't have bothered writing *that*. *That* was unlikely to be a problem. Pearl had never felt anything like the charged physical pull she and Tom felt towards each other. It would be enough to sustain them when they did not see eye to eye in other regards. Eleanor might as well have minded her own business. Yet again.

In the end, Tom's parents hadn't been able to attend the wedding anyway, though her parents and sister were there, and

Tom's brother, and one sister. The Mayfields couldn't come, they wired, because of the war; the fear was that the Banff Springs Hotel would be needed for some war-related purpose, and the doctor had better be around. And so Tom and Pearl were married, in January of 1941, in Montreal, and after the wedding they travelled to the Laurentians for their honeymoon ski trip.

Four years later, Pearl sat at her dressing table assessing herself, and her state, in the mirror. "You are trapped," she said. "How do you like that?" Gloomily, she picked up the silver-backed brush from her set. (Twelve pieces. Engraved. Sterling silver from Birks. A wedding present from her parents.) Immediately, her hands began warming the metal.

It was barely a month since she and Ruby had moved in with her parents, and things couldn't be going worse. On New Year's Day 1945, the day before Tom flew off to England with the RCAF, she and Ruby, two years old and devoid of sense, had taken the train from Regina to Calgary. Ruby had behaved badly the entire time and Pearl, who had so been looking forward to the trip, could have pitched her out the window without remorse. Her parents had met them at the station and brought them home. From the second her mother knelt down in front of Ruby and Ruby put her arms around her grandmother's neck and they cooed at each other and exchanged Eskimo kisses, Pearl knew that the arrangement was a bad idea. Her mother would try to take over and spoil the child.

But by then it was too late—she was a prisoner—and worse, she was in a prison of her own making. There would be no escape until Tom returned from England. It would be months. Could be years. Pearl heaved a great sigh. And to think she had done this to herself. Her mother would drive her around the bend before then, because she wouldn't stop meddling, and all too soon Pearl saw that her prediction was accurate: Opal was going to ruin Ruby. If Pearl announced a new policy she wanted implemented re child-rearing, her mother instantly met it with an argument as to its inefficacy.

Pearl brushed her hair. What right did her mother think she had to question her, the child's own mother, as to her tactics? Ten strokes. Just what did Opal think she could teach Pearl about being a mother? Twenty. It wasn't as if Opal had been an extraordinary mother herself. Look at her elder daughter—here, in the mirror. Was she on top of the world in any regard? Not likely. Thirty. Abandoned by her husband, saddled with a child. She bent over and dropped her head. Forty. Well, she would persevere in spite of her misgivings. What choice was there, really? Fifty. She sat up, tossed her head back, and put her silver-backed hairbrush down in its place with the rest of her boudoir set, patted it affectionately, and took up her nail file.

Being back here, in this house, in this room, she found herself responding and reacting to her parents as though she were twelve, or seventeen, not almost twenty-eight and a mother with a two-year-old. Speaking of which, Pearl could hear Ruby's juicy cough and her snorting and snuffling next door, along with the murmur of a voice that was either the maid's or Opal's. At least Ruby wasn't cranky with her cold: she liked taking her pink cough syrup, and she liked watching the steam coming out of the kettle in her room. No doubt her Gramma Opal was waiting on her hand and foot. Spoiling her even further.

(A week later, Pearl would come down with Ruby's cold, and she became much sicker with it than Ruby had been. She didn't leave her bed for a week. It didn't help matters that her mother's sickroom technique was deplorable: Pearl would ask for a glass of water and it might be half an hour before her mother would return. Or a handkerchief—once she'd ended up using a corner of the sheet, so then of course the bed had to be changed, and Pearl had to get out of bed and sit in a chair.)

Vigorously, Pearl filed her nails, creating a point on each one. To top off her misery, Tom's latest letter was a complete dud. It contained not one word of affection until he signed it "Love, Tom." And this, this one reference to love, was all he had to offer in a wedding-anniversary letter? Sure, greeting cards might be hard to come by in wartime, but words were free for the choosing. Why on earth did he think she would be interested in hearing what the editorial in the *Yorkshire Post* was about in the stead of endearments and words of love? Did he have rocks in his head? Or was their marriage old already, only three years on? Perhaps he had forgotten about her; perhaps he just didn't care, or surely to God he could use his imagination and visualize what her life looked like right now. Couldn't he tell that she had nothing to look forward to, to keep her spirits up, the way he did?

And the icing on the cake was that throughout her entire sickness and for three days beyond, not one single word from her husband. Not one, while she had managed to write once a day even when she could barely fill the pen. Ten days! How she hated having to depend upon him for her happiness. It wasn't fair. Or right. She couldn't *make* him write to her. She couldn't *make* him want to. When she thought about her helplessness, anger rose in her like lava, burning her heart, her throat, her words.

Valentine's Day came and went.

What was the matter with him, anyway? Here she was, a pitiable object, surely, to any feeling person. The postman came and went, came and went without anything for her day after day after day, until she couldn't bear the rejection any longer. She wrote the letter with the molten words that, given some of the things she said, he would construe as angry. She had written in a passionate fury, when she knew if she didn't do something she'd explode, at either Ruby or her mother. She'd slammed the door to her room and picked up a pen instead. Heat and power surged through her veins as she found her stride. How wonderful it felt to let the words gush from her completely unrestrained! She'd written an entire aerogram of tiny writing in half an hour. She had held nothing back, wrote direct from her heart and her head, and the two together reinforced her.

Her wretched situation was all his fault, she told him, for not writing her more often and for making such feeble attempts when he did. Was he afraid the censor might think he loved his wife if he wrote more than one special term of endearment in the salutation? She had begged him and begged him to write more often, and he had not. Why didn't she matter to him? Had he stopped loving her? If he had done what he was supposed to do, none of this would ever have happened and she would be happy for a change and all her letters to him would be sweet. She *did* matter, for his information.

She shouldn't have mailed it and she knew she shouldn't have mailed it. She'd ignored the cautioning voice in her head and made herself drop the letter in the box. Maybe she should have torn it up. But no: it was important to let him know what she was going through, because it at least gave him the opportunity to respond. And she did not hold with the notion some people had that when man and wife are far apart, some pieces of news would be better withheld, including, she supposed, the mental state of that wife. (Sometimes she wondered if she needed a psychiatrist. Should her husband know that? Yes. Especially when he was a doctor.) There was nothing to be gained by pretending that things were different than they actually were. It wasn't honest or useful, while even the exercise of pouring out misery in a few thousand words on paper could be of help, both to the person writing and to the intended recipient. She had felt so much better after writing. No, Tom would always get the straight goods from her. He might be in the war, but she wasn't going to deny the difficulties she was facing.

She looked sadly at herself in the mirror. She was angry yesterday, not today. Today she missed her darling husband with all her heart; loved him; longed for him. The only annoyance today so far was that she'd woken up with her period. Well, at least she wasn't pregnant. Odd, but with the onset of her menses she felt herself returning to a kind of calm, stability, after what she only now recognized as an emotional rather than rational state. It had happened before.

After Ruby was in bed that night, she wrote him again.

My Dearest Love,

I miss you so much tonight. I literally ache to have you near. I am infinitely wretched for every mile that separates us, and yet I am happy too, because I recognize myself tonight. The volcano has subsided and I am serene in the one thought, that I love you. I love you dear—ad infinitum. I want you to know that I am weeping mental tears of anguish when I recall the awful letter which will have reached you recently. I don't know what I can say except that I couldn't help my unhappiness, and I needed to share it with you, as you are my husband. I am sorry. Your letters (when you write) are so warm and nice and I deserve them so little.

I suppose I am just a poor weak female after all, with even less than the prescribed quota of spunk. I make a poor wife and mother. You can't say I didn't warn you, though, can you? You will remember my telling you quite clearly that I was never much interested in being married, because it did not look to me like a pleasant state. (I figured even then that I was probably poor material besides, though I never actually expressed this idea, even to myself.)

Let me share something with you, which might help explain things a little. From my earliest childhood my parents caused me a great deal of unhappiness one way and another, and permanently scarred me in some regards. When I left home for university and lived at McGill, I was able to rise above the warped sort of person I had been, and I felt a genuine personal triumph. Life seemed pretty good through those years—pretty straightforward, and comparatively carefree. I had escaped that unpleasant person I had been! And I swore a silent oath to myself that I would never again fall victim to the thousands of personality problems that ye gods now beset me again. *Here I am, a married woman with a child, living with my parents, up to my neck in memories of the unpleasant past. My one consolation—it almost makes it worth it—is my love for you.*

Tom, I wish, I must say, that we'd been more far-sighted when this plan to have me live here with my parents was hatched. I wish someone had told me that it would not work, because it won't. I have other regrets as well, and since I am in a confessional frame of mind, I will add that I wish we had waited to get married until after this war. I don't like your not being with me. With us. But you wouldn't have waited, I know. Or rather, your mother wouldn't have waited. But what can be done about it now? Nothing, as far as I can see.

I fear sometimes that I am vanishing. That my identity as an individual is almost gone. It's being taken from me at every turn. Let me quote you something I was reading recently, from The New Book of Etiquette *by Lillian Eichler. She says: "All women are addressed either as 'Mrs.' or 'Miss.' Mrs. Guy Scott is 'Mrs. Guy Scott,' not 'Mrs. Ellen Scott.' A widow remains 'Mrs. Guy Scott' and is addressed as such—never as 'Mrs. Ellen Scott.' A woman who has divorced her husband is still 'Mrs. Guy Scott' unless she prefers to call herself 'Mrs. Graf Scott,' her own name having been 'Ellen Graf.'" So you see, beloved husband, I lose my identity altogether by these rules no matter what the circumstances. Ask me not why.*

To be frank, Tom, I am in hell here. This is how bad things have become in only two months: My wretched mother says that I am obstinate and that you will certainly have to be some kind of a spineless nonentity to ever get along with someone so self-willed and inconsiderate as I upon your return. And she says that she hopes (this is the black curse) that Ruby will deal with me as heartlessly as I now do with my mother, and that I will suffer cruelly, as she now does.

I hope, if I am ever half as bad as she, you will promptly give me an overdose of something.

Love from your

Pearl

P.S. I am not an evil-minded person naturally.

Pearl placed her pen on the bedside table and slid down under the covers. She turned over her feather pillows and punched them, rolled over on her side and pulled the eiderdown quilt up around her ears. The pale green satin was cool against her cheek. After a few minutes she propped herself up on one elbow, reached for her mug and took a sip. The hot chocolate was cold. Irritation tightened her jaw. What *next*?!

One of Tom's sisters was getting married. Pearl and Ruby would go out to the wedding in Banff alone, on the train, while her parents drove out ahead in her father's latest car. May couldn't go—she was at university in Edmonton. Pearl would wear her navy suit and her pearls and last year's hat, while Ruby would be dressed like a miniature queen. Gramma Opal had bought her a pink coat with flowers embroidered on the collar, and a matching bonnet with a big satin bow to tie under her chin. Tom's mother had paid for new white shoes and stockings. Ruby would also have the first opportunity to wear the rabbit fur muff she had received for Christmas, even though it was March and it would be a miracle if there was still snow in Banff. Pearl hoped Ruby would evince some intelligence about the muff's use and not get it dirty. White was a ridiculous colour to put on a child. Well, if her hands were stuck in her muff, she couldn't very well suck her thumb, now, could she. All she did these days was suck one thumb and then the other.

Tom's father was at the station to meet them, and transported them to the Mayfield house on Buffalo Street, by the river. Her own parents were not there. The place was buzzing with excitement and activity. Eleanor Mayfield was in her element, bustling and bossing from here to there, some opinion to offer on everything. But she was gracious. The phone kept ringing—the church, the florist, the caterer from Calgary. Ruby trotted around happily, showing everyone her muff and her new white shoes, of which she was overly fond. Fortunately, everyone found her less annoying than sweet. Pearl settled in with a cup of tea, and heard the telephone ring again. Tom's sister Marjorie beckoned to her.

Pearl crossed the room and took the receiver. The call was from her father, at the Mount Royal Hotel. He blew right up. "Where are you?" he demanded. He knew when the train got in, he said, and he and her mother had expected her to show up with Ruby, and so they had waited. Why hadn't she gone straight to the hotel? Here he had made all the arrangements, he had paid for the room, and as a special treat he had engaged a suite for her and the child, and had she the common decency to show up? No, she had not. Had she the courtesy to telephone and say what had become of her? No, selfish wretch that she was, that she had always been, did she never think of anyone but herself? No, she did not, and now her mother was in a terrible state and that was Pearl's fault too, and since his own daughter was so utterly useless he would be left to deal with that as well, he supposed.

It was dreadful—standing there in the Mayfields' parlour, a smile pasted on her face, listening to him yelling on the telephone, trying to pretend there was nothing going on while he ripped her to shreds and no doubt everyone in the house could hear him. She tried to interrupt, tried to say that the telephone had been tied up, so she couldn't have called. But he was beyond reason. Finally, after he was finished with her, he hung up. She said, "Goodbye, Dad," into the dead receiver and went quickly to the bathroom. She sat down on a pale blue chair and held her face in her hands. How unstrung her father's anger had made her surprised her; heaven knew she ought to be used to it by now. What was the matter with her? It was just that he had been so even-tempered and amicable lately that she had let her guard down. That would teach her. As she sat there, safe now if horribly embarrassed, memories of the way she had felt as a child when he had assaulted her like that made her whole body begin to shake. Then came tears.

The next day, she and Ruby travelled with her parents from the hotel to the United church on the corner. The wedding itself went without a hitch. Ruby was overall well behaved during the service, if rather too conversational. Also, she had been quite taken by Gramma Mayfield's corsage and hat, and kept reaching over the back of the pew for them. She wouldn't sit down and behave, and she squealed if Pearl tried to make her, so Pearl held her in aching arms for much of the service.

Towards the end of March, Opal and Pearl spent an entire day working together, clearing out, cleaning and tidying what had once been the maid's room, when maids still lived in. They were turning it into a playroom for Ruby. Amazingly, mother and daughter had managed to work amicably together, agreeing on most things except on whether the window should be open or closed and whether the mat should be next to the door or the daybed. It was encouraging to know, even temporarily, that they didn't have to constantly bicker, they didn't even have to constantly talk. Each could do her job. Perform her task.

When they finished, around four, they called for the maid to bring Ruby up so they could surprise her. When Opal opened the door and said, "Ta-da!" Ruby just stood on the threshold. Pearl pushed her a little, but then Ruby clung to her grandmother's leg. Pearl tried and failed to pry her little fingers off. Then she started to get angry. Just who was in charge here? She gave up prying and tried to distract Ruby, showing her how her toys were all in the cupboards and drawers, but Ruby remained uncooperative. Talk about spoiled, thought Pearl, looking angrily at her mother and her daughter. The two of them together there, against her. There was little she could do about her mother, but Ruby—Ruby was hers, and as ungrateful a little wretch as you could imagine after all their work. "Like it or not, you are going to be in that room," Pearl said fiercely, and wrenched her daughter from her mother's leg. She set her down inside the room. "This is your playroom, Ruby, and you are going to stay in here and *play*." Ruby began to wail. Opal started towards her and Pearl shouted, "*No!*" and Opal stopped. Pearl closed the door quickly, leaving the child inside. "There!" she crowed, victorious. She turned the key in the lock. Ruby, crying, began trying to open the door. "Bye-bye, Ruby. Goodbye." Ruby started screaming blue murder and banging on the door. Pearl walked past her mother.

"Mummy! Mummy!" cried Ruby.

"Don't you dare let her out," Pearl hissed at Opal. At least, she thought as she descended the stairs and Ruby's cries grew muffled, they wouldn't have to hear her caterwauling when they were at dinner.

Pearl left the house and sat down on the front steps. The rain had stopped and the cold, damp air felt good. She was hot from all the fighting. Ye gods. What an ordeal. Damn her mother anyway. Did she *ever* do anything to support her daughter? No, she did not. Now Ruby would think that Gramma was wonderful and Mummy was not. That it was mean Mummy who locked her in the room, not wonderful Gramma. As though when Pearl was a child Opal herself hadn't locked her in her room, and *she* was the one wailing and crying. Opal never said, "Oh, the poor little thing" then, did she? The hypocrite.

Pearl

Two weeks later, Ruby still refused to play. Thankfully, she had ceased yelling when she was locked in her playroom and instead just stood at the door sucking her thumb. Pearl could see her through the keyhole. Pearl had tried going in to encourage her to play with her toys, but Ruby yelled and pushed them away so pettishly that Pearl soon gave up on that. Let her stew.

Tom,

For Ruby's sake as well as my own, I must *stay far away from the influences on which I blame most of my own unhappiness, and that is impossible while I am living here.* I swear to you on my life *that I shall* never again *consent to live anywhere near the wrangling of my mother and father. Everyone* wants *to love their parents. But from my mother I get nothing but castigation and criticism. Under her influence I am a nasty beast, and so is she. I feel no affection, only a searing sense of remorse that there is none. I have affection and respect for my father, but I cannot bear his unreasonableness and his rages.*

If anyone had told me four years ago that this would be how my life was going to pan out, I would have said I couldn't take it. My life is a mess. I know now why people occasionally take too many sleeping tablets.

Tom please *write to me something nice. Right now I desperately need the affection of someone. I am all alone here.*

Tell me—do you expect to come back soon *after Germany is attended to?*

P

If she had to stay living here until Tom got back, she'd kill someone, maybe herself. Something had to change. She had to get out of here. She was going in the wrong direction, away from her life, away from the life she was meant to be leading. This morning she had practically flayed Ruby alive for leaving her hairbrush on the floor. Now she hated herself. She *knew* that all she needed was some time to herself, but would anyone help her? If she had some time every day to be truly alone, she might be able to stand it. But no. This morning her mother had refused again to mind Ruby while Pearl went downtown. Now she heard Ruby murmuring outside her bedroom door. Damn her, and damn her thumb-sucking too. Some days she thought about just walking out on Ruby. Just putting on her coat and walking out that front door and into her life, the life that had been misplaced. The life she was meant to be living. Which wasn't this one. Certainly not this one. She wished she'd never had her.

She heard a soft knock. She didn't move a muscle.

Ruby knocked again. "Mummy?"

"Go away," said Pearl.

"Mummy? Gramma says—"

"Go away!"

Ruby started to cry. But at least she did what she was told, and the sound of her snivelling faded as she trotted down the hall.

Finally Pearl heard from Tom. He had received her terrible letters and loved her anyway, he said. He wasn't angry; she should know by now that he wasn't an angry sort of person. He said that he did indeed think of her in her desolate state and that he was sorry she was unhappy. He had been down in the doldrums himself, he said, and her loving letter—as opposed to her unloving one, she said to herself—had done much to boost his morale. Well, that was something, she supposed. But what would he do to *help* her?

A letter from her friend Marion came in the same mail. Dear, precious Marion made a casual yet monumental remark that would change the course of Pearl's destiny, give her hope, and bring light to her ever-darkening world. Marion said casually, commenting on Pearl's situation, about which she had been hearing a lot, "Well, Pearl, you could always come and live in Knowlton." Pearl's heart, *arising from sullen earth like the lark at break of day*, as she told her sister May, began to beat with excitement. Knowlton! Of course! Pearl knew Knowlton. She had been there. She had gone home with Marion one weekend and had found Knowlton to be a delightful place. She and Ruby could be happy there. They *would* be happy there. Why wouldn't they be? Oh, joy! What a tremendous, blessed relief it would be to leave all this behind. (And wouldn't that just fix her mother!)

Through further communications by letter and one or two secret phone calls, Pearl learned from Marion that she could rent a furnished house for between thirty and forty dollars a month. That there were women in town who did washing well and cheaply. That she could hire a man to stoke the furnace every night and morning and haul ashes for ten dollars a month. That some houses had electric stoves and that most had modern plumbing. That the local doctor was a graduate of McGill. Pearl got out her chequebook and a small notebook with a gold pencil and began to plan. And then she started a letter to her lord and master Tom, in which she would convey the results of her research and tell him that she was on the verge of defying his command and leaving Alberta. He could say aye or nay as he chose, but she had made up her mind.

April 20, 1945
Dear Tom,

I am so glad you have given your consent (as I do want you to be happy). The thought of leaving here sustains me through every day.

The robins and bluebirds have arrived here—very early. I hope, how I hope, it is spring where I am going, too. My trunk is partly packed.

Tonight I know that the accusation made by my mother that I am cold and unfeeling could not be further from the truth, to quote the sage. The fact is that I am a veritable blazing furnace. I swear I'll never again be able to bear the excitement of actual contact.

I miss you so much. How I long for the day we are reunited . . . in Quebec!

Oh darling, I love you so very, very much. Put your arms around me tight and hold me close. Mm-mm.

Love,

Pearl

P.S. Your parcel should reach you soon. The tins of sausages are from Mother.

All she had ever really wanted was her own way, and now that she all but had it, the skies were blue again. She had arranged to leave Calgary for Montreal on the train on May 1, spend a weekend in Montreal and then proceed to Knowlton on the Monday. Before long Tom would join them and then the three of them would live happily ever after. She knew it. What could possibly go wrong now?

She'd had a long talk with her father about her intended departure, and the air was much clearer between them. She had gone up to his study, where he had closed the door and offered her a glass of sherry. He knew how hard it was for her, he said. He knew what her mother could be like. He had been simply wonderful, and she had come away feeling happy. He had even offered to drive them to the station. But when she attempted to have a similar conversation with her mother, it was a miserable, horrid flop. Why had she hoped it might be otherwise? Ever since, Opal had been causing an awful stink and was impossible to get along with. She was mad at Pearl. She was mad at her husband. She was mad at Bill and Marge Black next door.

Three whole seasons before she would need winter clothes again. Now the sweaters and jackets were all in the trunk. Couldn't her mother see that it was in her best interests to be in Pearl's good books so that there would be a better chance of her coming home soon? (She *hadn't* told anyone, not even Tom, that this might well be permanent. She had decided to leave them with the impression that she was having an extended holiday. She hadn't told Tom's parents anything at all yet, but when she did—she would mail them a letter—she would tell them the same thing. When—or if—she decided she didn't like where she was, she would come back, and her parents would be glad to have her. And Ruby too, of course.)

Marge and Bill Black invited Pearl and her parents next door for a goodbye luncheon, to which she went alone as her mother was still having a spat with Marge over cooking with alcohol (putting wine in sauces, specifically), and before the meal was served Bill plied Pearl with so much Scotch she was in a pleasant haze for the remainder of the afternoon. How calm and happy she felt as she ambled home in the sunshine! Nothing got her riled. This, she supposed dreamily, lounging on the chesterfield in the living room, her head on a tasselled velvet cushion, was how alcoholics were made. It wasn't so much an addiction to alcohol, she decided, as an aversion to real life. Perhaps if she could keep herself well lubricated . . . and then she fell asleep.

The first night in their new home, Dr. and Mrs. Tom Mayfield stood together in the living room, raised their sherry glasses and proposed a toast to the future. The couple stood in profile as they lightly clinked the rims of their glasses together, Tom, Pearl and the fire all reflected in the tall plate glass windows behind them. Though they didn't speak of it directly, they both knew that the purchase of this house was intended to mark the end of many disappointments, and to be the start of a happier, more stable and prosperous time together.

"Here's to no more locums!" said Pearl.

"Here's to 'Home, Sweet Home,'" said Tom, and they kissed.

Pearl was almost six inches shorter than her husband, and while no one would ever call her fat, she liked to say, she might be called buxom. Still trim after two children. She was wearing a plaid box-pleated skirt and a round-neck sweater. Her amber clip-on earrings matched the simple string of beads around her neck. Tom, over six feet tall and almost too thin, was wearing a light grey suit that fit him loosely and was rumpled after a full day's work in his new practice with Dr. Strong. He still wore his tie, but he had loosened it. She took the sherry glass from Tom's hand and put the two glasses down on the mantelpiece. "Let's go and stoke the fire," she said. Then she lifted her eyebrows and he followed her up the two steps from the living room and down the hall.

The Tom Mayfields began their new life in the rural part of Beresford with a somewhat romantic vision of the pretty acreage they had bought from a family named Lightbody, who had been cured of that perception and had returned to the city. Tom and Pearl now owned ten acres of partially cleared land, where the Lightbody family had planted an orchard and built a long, low house for themselves room by room as they could afford to (the pre-plumbing outhouse was still standing twenty yards or so from the house). The house stood on the edge of a ravine that led down through mature fir and cedar trees to a healthy brown creek with wildflowers and vine maples thriving along its banks, skunk cabbages in its mud. A fallen tree served as a bridge. More forest lay beyond. Outside the living room windows, a black walnut tree thrived in the middle of an uneven, intermittently green lawn. The whole property seemed perfect, even idyllic, and their two daughters, Ruby and Laurel, twelve and six, both loved it, loved the grass, the apple trees, the wildflowers. Ruby disappeared into the woods to read a book; Laurel disappeared to climb trees.

Small brown rabbits peeked out from the ferns. Birds chirped in the trees. It was a setting from D.H. Lawrence, thought Pearl, as she undressed with her back to her husband. And anticipated with pleasure the feel of his naked body against hers, his lean, cool torso, his strong fingers. Their bodies drew them together in expressions of love more than anything else—if that's what their intermittent commingling was these days. Their communication was otherwise poor, but in this, *this*, their communication was direct, and strong, and pure, and they were close, loving, as they lay together afterwards. That all changed as soon as they stood up.

It was a rude shock to both of them when, before a year had passed, they realized how much work the acreage was going to be. Tom, concentrating on the world beyond the driveway—establishing his practice, learning the hospital routines, meeting new patients—worked long hours and was often out on calls in the night as well. He felt unable and unwilling to address anything else. He had reached his capacity, he said when she complained he was no help; she would have to pick up the slack. Pearl stayed home with their three daughters (Amethyst was born nine months after they moved in), six months pregnant with yet another, unplanned.

All too quickly Pearl had realized just how isolated they were from like-minded people and how ridiculous the romantic vision she and Tom had shared had been. Instead of lambs frolicking in fields while a shepherd and shepherdess made floral crowns for each other under a blue sky with white, fluffy clouds that Wordsworth might have enjoyed describing, there was a dirty, uncouth man in coveralls and a yellow slicker out in the pouring rain digging up the septic field with a backhoe for the third time.

In addition to the septic field problems, the motor that pumped water up to the house from the creek kept stopping and needing priming, so finally a well had to be dug and paid for. The furnace broke down and had to be replaced. The soil in the gardens was terrible, and Pearl could not make anything grow no matter how hard she worked, when she could, that is, which wasn't often, plagued as she was with all the children.

Dr. Strong had turned out to be a coarse, vulgar, drinking man who was quite different in person than on the page. His wife spent her afternoons in the beer parlour. Medicine was apparently not enough for Dr. Strong, because he also kept cows and farmed on the side. "Imagine!" said Pearl, and told her sister May the story Tom had told her at the dinner table in an attempt at conversation. Tom had reported that Strong had worn his manure-laden gumboots right into the operating theatre to deliver a baby. Likely, Tom had added, in the same way he might deliver a cow of her calf. And then Tom had told a joke, which she shared with May. "Did you hear the one about the man who was training his horse to go without food? It was going really well but then the horse up and died."

"Ha ha," said May. "The poor horse!"

"That's the kind of humour my husband finds funny. I doubt he could read it as a metaphor, however, which is too bad."

Pearl didn't confide to May that she had started to feel little waves of panic as though she were going to drown. The waves came when she had nothing left to give, when she was on her last legs, and yet still more was demanded of her. Nothing was ever enough for any of them. She always, it seemed, could hear one if not two children crying. "Leave me alone!" she cried, covering her ears. No one noticed her despair, no one cared. Tom was conveniently absent when the time came to deal with any and all of the problems. Their children demanded constant attention and offered nothing in return but more demands. Her parents harangued her for not writing. Everyone wanted something of her and no one gave back a thing. Ye gods. What kind of life was this turning out to be?

"But are you overall happy in Beresford, Pearl? I so hoped you would be happy there," said May. "You thought you would be."

"Well, if it were up to me, I would be," Pearl retorted. "Or if I could get any help around here." No doubt, she said, May's husband Fred was a bigger help to May. Lucky her. Here *she* was, with no help of any description, as anyone who wasn't blind could see if he actually wanted to, stuck in a rural neighbourhood six miles from the hick town of Beresford, a neighbourhood that was filled to the brim with uneducated people who either did not work at all or were labourers and small-time farmers whose wives spent their days doing who knew what. Gathering eggs. Making bread.

"Ah," said May.

"And who, anywhere within fifty miles," Pearl asked May, "would not look at me blankly if I said something like *Many people would sooner die than think*? Or if I said, *Too little liberty brings stagnation*, who would nod knowingly, and engage in conversation?"

"*I* might look at you blankly," said May.

"But you know what I mean."

"I suppose I do," said May. "But Pearl, there's Fred home from choir. I haven't got his tea on."

"Well, you had better go wait on him hand and foot, then, hadn't you?"

At first, Pearl had made half-hearted attempts to befriend the wives of other professional men, but these times were rare because usually Tom had the car. But she felt it was her duty as a doctor's wife to make the effort. Tom expected that she would associate with these women, as his darling mother would do, take to their level of social discourse like a duck to water. Pam Carpenter. Loretta Nielson. But she had no desire to talk about meatloaf recipes, or the PTA. She did not want to talk about church plays and teas or to serve on committees. She was not being pretentious, as he had accused her of being; it was just that her frame of reference was different. Her scope was broader. She wanted to go home the moment she arrived at their homes, even as she stood rigid with tension ringing the doorbell with a false smile pasted on her red lips. So she stopped trying before she had really started; what she had to endure along with the pretence was hardly worth the effort. She had better things to do with her time.

She could not look to her children as a source of intelligent conversation either. The way they nattered on endlessly, it would be ridiculous to suppose children were capable of much in the way of dialogue. At best they were parasites, threatening to suck her dry with their constant demands. Mummy this, Mummy that, all day long. It made her skin crawl sometimes until she wanted to scream. And sometimes she did. To her it defied logic, but the less she offered them, the more they wanted. Why couldn't they get the message?

Vivien, daughter number four, was conceived when quick nighttime couplings were all that remained of Pearl and Tom's once intense and fiery relationship in bed. When Pearl had discovered that she was pregnant again, she cried for days. Would she *never* be free? She sat at her dressing table and looked at her sad, weary face. How in heaven's name had she got here? How could she ever extricate herself from this? Her life—her body, her mind—would never be her own again.

The ransom she demanded of Tom from then on for sex became so high that Tom wouldn't pay it, and he no longer approached her in the night. If he attempted to kiss her hello or goodbye, she turned her face from him. She believed he didn't want her enough to do even the smallest thing she begged of him, even if it meant he got sex in return, something he had always wanted. That's how far gone they were, she wailed, that's how much he didn't want her anymore. He was silent. So the fourth baby—ye gods, another girl—came home to air that was thick with anger and resentment. A steady stream of disappointment emanated from both her parents. Pearl's nighttime wailing and crying startled the newborn baby awake and into crying and made sleep restless for the other three children, as they felt anger's reverberations in every breath they drew into their soft, clean lungs.

What a crew her children were, all yammering and in the way every second. More unsatisfying work she had never done; she would rather her liver were plucked out every day. Ruby, the eldest, was an uncommunicative child who did her utmost to avoid helping and stood there like a dumb thing when she was asked a question. Pearl wondered if she was slow, though Tom insisted she was not. Her report cards from school praised her high intelligence. But why, then, did she stare so stupidly at her mother when she was told what to do? As though she barely comprehended, or did not at all.

"Don't you hear me? I *said*, rock Vivien's carriage."

Ruby, lost in her thoughts, didn't move. Pearl spoke more loudly.

"Didn't. You. Hear. What. I. Said? Why are you standing there! Are you stupid? Now listen to your sister wailing. Look what you've done. Go away. Fat lot of help you are."

Laurel, a handful for her teachers because she would not sit still or be quiet, lacked focus, was both flighty and belligerent, and was no help either. She ran off at the first sign of trouble, most of it caused by her own thoughtlessness and carelessness. And the two little ones—Amy, with asthma and allergies and a ceaseless appetite, and Vivien, underweight and such a crybaby she wouldn't eat or shut her trap unless she were constantly held, and ye gods, who had time for that? What cruel cosmic joke was the universe playing on her, plaguing her with such a crew?

And then there was of course her husband. She was provoked beyond endurance by him, by the inane, dreamy expression on his face and his retreat into silence when confronted; by his withdrawal; by his refusal to give a straight answer, an intelligent answer, *any* answer at all. Damn him anyway! Was she going to be trapped forever by lamebrains? Yes.

But she would not quit even if she could. *She* stuck things out to their conclusions, she said to him. She was like her father, whom she admired enormously, unlike *some people* she could name who never got anything much going at home. And whatever it was he did at work, it *didn't* involve making enough money to feed their family or to fix all the things that went wrong. What kind of a useless man had she married?

"Useless, am I," said Tom. "I see."

Pearl sighed the heavy sighs of a martyr and she took the yardstick to her children when her hands got tired from spanking. *Someone* had to bring up their four. She would resign herself to what was apparently fated to be her mission in life: raising selfish children and feeding a useless, *yes*, a useless husband. Year after year after year. She brushed her hair with her silver-backed brush every night and every morning. She did thirty sit-ups and ten deep-breathing exercises. She gardened, though her success with plants was as hard to see as her success with her children. She spent hours digging and weeding, but nothing seemed to help what was, she determined, basically inferior soil.

As far as the children went, she would raise them right. She was made of Scottish stuff, at least on her father's side. With her father's grim determination, daring anyone to find fault, she consulted Canada's Food Guide and balanced her daughters' protein, carbohydrate, vegetable and fruit intakes. Supper was on the dining room table every night at six o'clock sharp, and if you weren't there you didn't get fed. Pot roast or pork chops fried in the cast iron pan; macaroni and cheese baked in the oven; chicken stew with dumplings bubbling on the stove; potatoes and carrots cooked in the pressure cooker. Canned peas and canned wax beans, canned asparagus and canned corn; canned pears, canned peaches, or Jell-O with rubbery edges, and peanut butter or chocolate chip cookies. All served on a matching set of Melmac dishes except on Sundays, when the table had a cloth and was set with the hand-painted Wedgwood wedding china, each piece ever so slightly different yet at first glance the same. What a garden of a life those flowers had once suggested. Ha. She scrubbed the pots and ran the dishwasher when it was working, and when it wasn't, she washed all the dishes, too. And if there was half an hour at the end of the day for her to read a book, more often than not she was too exhausted to read much beyond a page, and what she read—de Beauvoir, Sartre—made her more, not less, unhappy with her lot.

When Tom came home and she laid into him for being late, for abandoning his family to lead his pleasant and charming life in the outside world, he turned on his heel without stopping and left the house. She followed him. She took pleasure in goading him; at least something to do with him made her feel good. "Where are you going now? What's wrong with us all, that you can't bear to be in the same house with your own wife and offspring? Tom? Tom!" She could see Amy and Vivien, four and three, peering out their bedroom window. They watched as their father got back in his car, backed into the turnaround, and drove off in the rain and snow.

Occasionally, as the years passed, there were signs, hopeful indications that didn't all end in disappointment, though most still did. After much prodding, for example, Tom had finally located enough inner fortitude to part ways with Strong and open his own practice. This move resulted in more money, and the purchase of a second car, which gave Pearl more freedom. She was able to hire a young man to help her with the garden. He cut and cleared branches, cleaned the eavestroughs, mowed the lawn, and dug manure and peat moss into the gardens, which then improved. And a cleaning woman, Irma Olsen, now came in once a week. Let her get down on her hands and knees to wash and wax the floors. Let her clean the bathroom and dust. At least Irma would be getting paid. Money. If only she too could have some money of her own, if only she didn't have to ask her husband if she could please, please have two nickels to rub together. What a difference that would make.

No other man in the neighbourhood went off to work wearing Dack's shoes and a tailored suit and tie over a professionally pressed white shirt. If men went to work at all—many of them didn't—they went in work clothes: coveralls, or dark green pants and shirts, or blue jeans and plaid flannel work shirts. One fellow fixed radios and TVs in his garage. Another had fourteen dairy cows that occasionally pushed down the fence and trespassed on the Mayfields' land. The children from the families whose parents did not work didn't have much in their school lunches; Laurel reported that the kids in the family on the left of them were sent off to school with glass jars of water, and apples or pears stolen from the Mayfields' orchard, in big brown paper bags with the tops rolled down, or in plastic bread bags.

"You ungrateful wretches don't know how fortunate you are," Pearl told her three remaining children as she drove them to their lessons. Ruby had by now graduated from high school and miraculously landed a scholarship to attend university in California. "Just look around you at all the children who have so much less. Look at the Babcocks up the hill, all ten of them impoverished both physically and mentally. Look at the Whites next door, and the Jensons up near the school. You four have so much to be grateful for, and instead you're always whining, and selfish." She shook her head in disgust as she gripped the steering wheel of the station wagon with both hands. "If you turn out badly, believe you me, the blame cannot fairly be placed on me."

But more money didn't translate into more peace or happiness for long. Getting a little relief only illustrated how much more was needed. Pearl had thought Ruby little more than a millstone but she must have been of some help, as she was, on occasion, missed. Pearl had broken down and asked her parents for money more than once, and they had obliged, but the last time she asked, her father had said no. The shame she felt at being denied translated into more anger at Tom for putting her in such a humiliating position. In the evenings, when he got home, they collided within minutes—why was he always late? He always had some excuse. Over and over again they separated, collided again, ignoring, accusing, jabbing, always ending with cold, hard silence, followed by Tom's retreat to the piano. There was tension *before* he walked in the door, in fact; he ignited it like a match to propane first with his foolish and futile attempts at a cheerful greeting as he came in and then with his attempts to ignore her. He wasn't going to get off easily if she had anything to say about it.

One day she found she couldn't wait, and she met him in the carport, stood waiting for him to get out of his car and followed him into the house. "How *dare* you maintain a pretence of happiness?" Pearl lashed out. "Waltzing in here without a care in the world when I am fed up to the teeth from slaving all day for you."

Tom, who had started having a couple of drinks before coming home, closed the closet door and turned to her. "Pearl, you at least have been on your own all day, while *I*'ve been surrounded by *sick people*, people to whom you wouldn't give the time of day. You might remember that, before you complain about everything so strenuously." Pearl tried to interject, but he held up his hand. "The people I see every day all want something of me," he continued quietly and coldly, "and some of them—a good too many of them, actually—are of a kind I do not relish and would not choose as company. Some of them smell, quite frankly. But I have no choice, these people are my patients, and they are my duty as well as my—and your, if you need reminding—bread and butter."

"Ha," said Pearl.

"What, if I may ask," said Tom, "do you consider *your* duty if it isn't your home and family?"

"For the record," she said as he stopped talking and attempted to move past her, "I have not been alone *all day*. For too much of the day, in fact, I've been surrounded by little wretches who want something from me *all the time*. I'd be happy to trade you any day. They're your children too, remember, or have you forgotten?"

Tom looked over her shoulder at his piano. "Excuse me," he said to Pearl.

Pearl's voice changed. "Oh, Tom," she beseeched, clutching his arm. "Please wait, just for a minute? Couldn't you please, *please* for *one second* appreciate how hard it is for me? Don't you *ever* attempt to see things from where I stand?"

Tom yanked his arm away from her. "You are standing in the way," he said, and walked around her and sat down on the piano bench. He placed his hands lightly on his thighs. He bent his head.

"No," she said. "No, you don't, damn you anyway." Her voice rose in anger as she stood on the top step and looked down at him. "The extent to which you don't care is abundantly clear. Just look at you at that damned piano." Tom lifted his hands to the keyboard and began playing. Major scales. Minor scales. Quickly, and loud. Next, the Bartók. Or the new one, the one by Dave Brubeck.

If she had time in the evenings after the supper dishes were done—and as the children grew, she was able to find half an hour or an hour more often—Pearl knit sweaters for herself. She did not knit as well as her sister, she knew, but she enjoyed it when she was too tired to read, and she counted it as something she did for herself. Too, the results of knitting were tangible, satisfying, and unlike domestic work, knitting stayed done for more than ten minutes and even garnered occasional praise. These days she could find more time to read, too, and as well as de Beauvoir and Sartre she was reading Thomas Hardy, Virginia Woolf, Beckett.

She tried to resume contact with her university girlfriends who, like her, were raising young families, but neither she nor they really had time to correspond beyond notes on Christmas cards. Pearl had more than once made what she considered valiant efforts and written them each three- or four-page letters. But her attempts seldom gleaned a reply even from Marion, never from Esther, and she felt shunned. Who cared if she lived or died? Anything was more important than she was. She was abandoned. Unloved. Pain easily turned into anger, which coursed hotly through her body. To outward appearances she looked cold, and hard, and aloofly self-contained, but inwardly she seethed. The anger followed familiar paths.

No one cared an iota except perhaps little Amethyst, now in school and who, if she were coaxed, would kiss her mother even after she'd been thrashed, though it was hard to tell anymore if she was motivated more by greed than by genuine affection for her mother. But at least she would do as she was told. And Amethyst was the only one who didn't argue or cast her injured, baleful looks. She said, "Yes, Mummy. Okay Mum," and her bed was always made and her homework was always done, though she seldom laughed, and always looked somewhat worried. She, one out of four, was fine, except for excessive snuffling from the allergies, and she earned the rewards that came her way, her clothes and her cookies and ice cream, though Pearl continued to have some concerns over the excessive eating. As a toddler, Amy had gone off to visit the neighbours and there she had begged for food. Begging food! Pearl had spanked her thoroughly and then pinned a note to the back of her shirt where she couldn't reach it: *Do Not Feed Me.* In what was surely a show of spite, Amy had now taken to eating her hands—chewing her nails down to the quick—and sneaking food from the refrigerator. And so it was no wonder Amethyst was plump, while Vivien, who seemed barely to eat, was so thin.

The snow was turning to sleet by the time Tom came home one day in mid-December; his car made fresh tracks in the driveway. His supper was waiting for him on the kitchen table, cold and congealing. Pearl opened the front door to confront him, but when he saw her there, he turned around and headed back to his car.

"Where are you going now?" she said.

"I don't need this," said Tom, and he closed his car door, backed into the turnaround and drove off in the sleet, making a second set of tracks over and beside the first, weaving in and out, combining and separating.

"What kind of Christmas is this going to be?" she called after him. "Tom? Tom!"

After the car's tail lights disappeared, Pearl slammed the front door. She stormed into Ruby's bedroom and shut the door behind her. Ruby, nineteen, looked up in fear from her book. "About Christmas," Pearl said. "I'm telling your grandparents not to come after all. It isn't convenient. They can go somewhere else." Ruby looked at her. "You know, I've about had it with the whole shiftless lot of you. You are out of your minds if you think I am going to play Santa on top of everything else. See how you all like *that*."

Ruby asked her mother in a whisper who *was* going to be Santa then. Pearl said that she didn't know and she didn't care. "Ask your father," she said. "*He* has all the answers."

But Tom wasn't around the next day or the next. He was busy at Christmas, Ruby knew. All the doctors were. There were so many car accidents, there were so many drunks driving and getting into fights.

Ruby was worried about trying to be Santa all by herself, but she worried about asking Laurel to help her because Laurel, at thirteen, might still believe in Santa. And even if Laurel didn't still believe in Santa, Ruby worried that it would upset her to hear how their mother was refusing to do it. But above all she was worried that she couldn't do it right herself. So she told Laurel anyway, and on Christmas Eve, when Tom was out on a call and Amy and Vivien were in bed and who knew where their mother was, they filled the stockings and wrapped the presents from Santa that Pearl had bought before she got angry and quit and which were stored in big shopping bags in her closet. Ruby felt guilty the whole time, as though she and Laurel were doing something they weren't supposed to do. Laurel cried and cried and Ruby said couldn't she please, please stop. But Laurel was a little sister herself, and couldn't.

Pearl was well aware that Tom was an attractive man. She knew too that some of his traits—the ambiguity, the never quite saying no, or yes—were appealing to a certain kind of woman. The kind who didn't care if he ever took any initiative or made up his mind. He could seem, she knew, to be charming and intelligent while actually being vague and indecisive. Some women could attribute desirable traits to him in light of his quiet good looks and warm, unreadable smile. Some women seemed able to detect a gentle vulnerability in Tom Mayfield that Pearl identified as spinelessness, and to forgive him everything, while she forgave him nothing.

His four daughters worshipped him—which was easy to do when he was as remote as a god on Olympus—while she, she was therefore unfairly cast as a harridan from Hades. Vivien was the worst. When Pearl sent her outdoors to play before supper, out the kitchen window Pearl could see her wandering up and down the driveway, and if the window were open she could hear her making up her ridiculous cowboy songs as she waited for her precious father to arrive home. The songs were as ingenuous as her view of him; she naively imagined him as a hero out in the world healing and saving people. Well, let her have a man like Tom when she married. Let that be her curse. *That* would cure her romanticism.

There was the business between Tom and that ridiculous woman at the corner store. Etta Carson. She and her husband ran the IGA; Etta was the cashier and Roy was the stock boy and butcher. They didn't have children, and they lived upstairs at the back of the store. The Carsons were friends with Irma, the cleaning lady, and her husband, a house painter named Joe. This arrangement was handy and useful to Etta, Pearl reported to May, because Etta was always so eager for news about Dr. Mayfield. It was Etta, she said, who began leaving unsigned cards and letters for Tom in the mailbox, and when Pearl was the one who went down for the morning mail and found the notes, she read them and then took pleasure in making great fun of Etta by reading selections aloud at the dinner table. "Oh my," she might say. "This one reeks of what must be Evening in Paris. Afternoon in Beresford would be more like it, though, wouldn't it? Smelling faintly of mushroom compost? Is it having the desired effect on you, Tom? Are you going to have to nip out to the store for cigarettes?"

The three girls watched with uneasy interest as their mother provoked their father. Laurel kicked the rungs of her chair. "Sit still," said Pearl. Laurel slipped down in her chair until her eyes were at table level. "You sit up this instant," said Pearl. Amethyst was next. Even if Amethyst *appeared* to be still and quiet, beneath the table Pearl knew she was tapping the ends of her shoes together, and her fingers were fidgeting and twitching. She likely had an extra dinner bun in her lap, too, the little thief, saving it for later. So Pearl glowered at her and predictably she started to snuffle. Pearl heaved a sigh. And Vivien? She was staring angrily at her plate as though she were trying to break it with her gaze. No doubt wishing Pearl would leave her wonderful father alone. How little she knew. Even the old dog Jake, who lay otherwise motionless in front of the fireplace, ever hopeful that someday there would be another fire in the grate to warm his old black and white body, had one ear cocked for the sound of danger. It floated in the air, made his nostrils and eyelids flicker.

Pearl touched her lips with her serviette. "I have something further on the subject to share that may be of interest," she said. "The *pièce de résistance.* If I may have your full attention." And she took the letter from its envelope. "You simply must listen to this. It is priceless. This time she's written, 'My heart beats at the thought of you.' Only she has spelled it b-e-e-t-s. Beets! That woman has such colourful prose. And she has included a pressed flower from her garden. Isn't that sweet."

Tom muttered something about "unkind."

"Unkind." Pearl laughed bitterly. "Well, you ought to know about that. I will pass this missive around now, so that you all can see. Laurel, you can clear the table. Laurel! Do as you're told!"

After a long, tense silence filled with the clatter of plates on the kitchen counter and a crash on the floor as Laurel dropped a glass, Tom said, "Did you hear what Pearson had to say today?"

Pearl stared at him, nonplussed. Then she said, as though she had been waiting for the opportunity, "I have no sense of the world beyond the laundry room door."

One Sunday night in June, the telephone rang and it was Roy Carson calling from the IGA to say that he'd found Jake, dead, hit by a car, in the ditch across from their store. Mr. Carson had seen him when he was sweeping the lot after closing up for the night.

Tom located a large empty sack in the garden shed and rounded up Laurel, Amethyst and Vivien, and together they walked to the corner.

As the four of them turned back up the driveway carrying Jake's body, Tom carrying two corners and Laurel two and the little girls traipsing behind, Pearl watched them from the kitchen window. Then she came out the back door and down the steps into the carport just as Tom and Laurel were laying the dog down on the cement slab. Amethyst and Vivien stood beside their silent father, tears streaming down their small, miserable faces, watching, watching. Laurel continued to sob quietly as she patted Jake goodbye and then turned away, leaned against one of the wooden posts. "Poor old boy," Pearl said sadly, her voice oddly gentle as she crouched down and stroked the dog. *"Jake's fate I mourn; poor Jake is now no more, / Ye Muses mourn, ye chamber-maids deplore."* She added softly, "My poor old fellow," and stood up, while Vivien pushed up closer against Amy, wiping her snot and her tears on her sister's shoulder.

Week after week, Pearl shopped for groceries at the Co-op and straightened the house, supervised the cleaning woman and cooked, angrily and without enthusiasm. Jamming the spatula down on the fried ham. Peeling the potatoes so that the peels flew. Kitchen work was too obvious a part of her "domestic bondage," she told May, which she was learning more about through her reading. Besides, she simply *did not like* to cook, and was there something so terribly wrong with that? No, there wasn't, May wrote back, though your family do have to eat, and who else is there but you to feed them? "Why do you never take my side?" Pearl countered. "People without children are the first to offer stupid commentary."

She did not consider herself an impulsive person, but one day she acted like one: she stopped at a driveway where a cardboard sign advertised puppies for sale. "I must be out of my mind," she thought, but she brought two of them home in a box. As if she needed more work to do. But she missed having a dog around, there had always been a dog when she was growing up, and perhaps this would end some unhappiness. The pure black puppies were both males, and would be less trouble than females. She named them Wayne and Shuster, and told the girls they would keep them as long as they were willing to help. It was only Vivien who really took to them; she spent hours on her stomach playing with them and chatting away as if they could understand her. But Vivien was an unreliable and inconsistent caregiver of herself as well as others. She forgot to wear her undershirt, she forgot to close the door behind her when she left the house. One day she had taken the puppies down to the creek without permission and one of them had fallen in off the log that crossed the water and Vivien had gone in after it and the two of them were soaked and half drowned by the time they got back to the house.

In the mornings, while Tom practised the piano, Pearl got the girls up, supervised their dressing and washing and brushing, and herded them into the kitchen, where they sat down at their places for breakfast. A multivitamin was placed on each of the three bread-and-butter plates beside a glass of juice or a pared grapefruit or a quartered orange. Pablum for the almost six-year-old Vivien, and one of four different kinds of porridge for the others spooned into bowls and a watchful eye kept on how much sugar each girl used, especially Amethyst, who would empty the bowl if you let her. Clean, neat and tidy, with lunch kits and satchels, and plenty of time to walk to the bus stop at the corner, they were thrust out the back door and Pearl closed it firmly behind Laurel and Amethyst. One more to go. Vivien. Who clearly longed to go with her sisters but instead remained at home, playing with her dolls, playing with the dogs, practising her reading. Drawing. Keeping quiet and out of her mother's way.

Laurel was unruly, loud and belligerent, and she still lied and cried in turn or at once at the least purported offence. Amethyst was still obedient but with that tendency to fidget, to bite her nails and to eat, and finally Vivien, thin and boyish, was either clinging to the house like a limpet or running off to play down at the creek.

It was Wayne, not Shuster, who started catching chickens at the neighbour's, and a solution had to be found or that neighbour threatened to use the shotgun. Pearl consulted her father. She then asked the neighbour for one of the dead birds and she tied it securely around the dog's neck with baling twine. The carcass, which stank worse with every passing day, stayed attached to the dog's neck until it rotted off. No one, not even Shuster, would go near him. Pearl felt a pulse of compassion as she looked at the sad, humiliated dog as he lay alone on a sack in the woodshed, but she repressed it. He had to learn, or he would lose his life. The children seemed unable to get the picture. "*Please* take the chicken off, Mum? Please, Mum, *please*?"

"No. Be quiet."

Tom said nothing. And her strategy worked: the dog never went after another chicken.

Vivien's first day of school was a monumental day for Pearl. She had been waiting years for this day, the day she would finally have the house to herself from September to June. Hallelujah! She expected to be filled with unquenchable joy. Yet while she knelt to do up Vivien's cardigan, she felt instead a tidal wave of deep sadness sweep through her so strongly that she gasped. She stopped, and Vivien, wondering, looked at her. Pearl smoothed the shoulders of the sweater, feeling the child's bones beneath it. She turned up the cuffs once more before she got to her feet and ushered the three of them out into the world, shutting the door behind them. "Goodbye," she said.

Turning away from the window and leaning up against the door, Pearl thought to herself: Freedom! But she felt bereft, not liberated. Why? she asked herself. What was the matter now? Why did she feel loss, not gain? Her chest seized up and her breath was rapid and shallow. The house was silent. The dogs quiet. Leaning up against the closed door, Pearl knew she was the one who had to do something about her life, because no one else was going to help her. But how? How was she to do this? She slid down against the door and wept, her head resting on her knees. What, oh what, was she going to do? What did she even *want* to do, now that she could? All that longing, all that waiting, but she had no plan. This blank slate, this empty canvas, this closed open door, and all she felt was panic.

Pearl preferred her parents safely confined to the silver frames on her dressing table, but she couldn't *always* dissuade them from coming. She did not enjoy their visits, and as the day of their arrival approached, the pressure inside her grew. She felt like a pinball inside. She knew she became more unreasonable and unpredictable in her criticisms and demands, and that it didn't endear her to anyone. But nothing in the house was right. Why did her parents have to come at Christmastime? They had just been here at Easter and again in August. Look at the house. Everything was a shambles. She was a terrible housekeeper and she knew it, and everyone else knew it too, but she was still expected to do a good job.

On the day her parents arrived, Pearl left the older two girls at home—Ruby had arrived home from California on the bus—and loaded Amy and Vivien into the car and drove into Vancouver, where Opal and Mac were waiting outside the train station with their luggage. No doubt they were irked at her tardiness, Pearl said as she parked the car. Well, that was just too bad. They could bally well wait.

Her mother stood sturdily and patiently, short-gloved hands holding her handbag in front of her. She wore a hat with black netting that fell elegantly over her face, and the bodies of dead mink were draped around the shoulders of her black wool coat. Those dead animals made Pearl's skin crawl. Beneath was her travelling dress, navy blue with tiny white dots, and on her feet were her shiny black lace-up grandma shoes with the tiny holes poked through in patterns.

Underneath the hat's netting Opal's face was worried, no doubt, though once she saw her granddaughters approaching at a run, a warm smile spread across her face and she opened her arms wide. Oh my dearies! she exclaimed. It's so good to *see* you! And they, so happy to be her *dear little girls*, instead of *her* miserable wretches, no doubt, rushed into her arms, and kissed her, breathing in the smell of her face powder and cologne. They had never greeted *her* so, thought Pearl. Their faces never lit up at the sight of *her*.

Pearl's father, ever the CPR lawyer, always dressed for the occasion (he even packed to dress for dinner at the fishing lodge). He wore a double-breasted suit and tie, and stood straight as a stick beside his wife. Under his hat his hair was straight, short and silvery white. His mouth was like Pearl's: straight as an arrow, and tight. He never hugged or kissed Pearl or the granddaughters, and he encouraged them to do the same.

"You're late, Pearl," he greeted Pearl.

"Hello, Dad," said Pearl. "Hello, Mother."

After the drive out to Beresford, her mother's first concern was with the baking she had sent ahead. Had it all arrived? Was it in crumbs? They had better check. Amy and Vivien carried the boxes in from the back porch, where they were stored beside the selection of Dutch cheeses a patient had given Tom as payment. Pearl watched her mother snip the string and take off the brown paper wrapping. Carefully, she lifted out the pretty tins and opened the lids to reveal the fancy baking, baking she learned to do from *her* mother in Winnipeg, she told her granddaughters, and would teach them to do too, if they liked, and if they were good, which she was sure they were. (Ha, thought Pearl.) The younger two's watering mouths opened and shut with wild desire as they pushed up against their grandmother's warm, soft body and she tucked her peppermint "sweeties" into their mouths. Pearl turned her back, returned to the dishes.

Unlike her, her mother liked being in the kitchen, and she sat her granddaughters on stools and taught them to make ginger muffins, to put the half cup of oil into the measuring cup first and then the molasses so that the latter slipped out cleanly. She taught them to cut in butter, and to roll pastry dough out lightly so it wouldn't be tough. They learned to sift and to measure, with spoons and a knife, and they made hearts and stars and gingerbread men with raisin eyes. All things she had once tried to teach Pearl, Pearl remembered, but Pearl had resisted mightily. May was a much better candidate for future domestic servitude, for becoming a domestic drudge. Opal sang under her breath as she made the soft white buns for their Christmas dinner, teaching the girls to knead and pluck the dough. Prepared them to look after men. There would be no progress for women as long as there were women like her mother around.

In the evening, her father and Tom attempted polite conversation as they shared a Scotch in the living room, but it faltered quickly. During the previous year's visit, her father had sided with Diefenbaker on the Cuban Missile Crisis, Tom with Kennedy, and there hadn't been much common ground there or anywhere else. Neither one of them had forgotten that and so they soon escaped to reading, Tom to *Clavier*, her father to a thick tome like Samuel Clarke's *The Life and Death of Hannibal, the Great Captain of the Carthaginians.* Pearl and her mother sat side by side on the loveseat, knitting. In between rows Pearl calculated the hours until she dropped her parents back at the station, the hours until her parents would leave her in peace.

Her parents died a year apart, her father in April 1964, her mother the following summer. May was devastated each time, but not Pearl. For the longest time the deaths seemed to be something she had made up, or dreamt, and she wondered at herself for not feeling anything much, no waves of sorrow, no great loss. Not even for her father. Perhaps the grief would come later? Perhaps, as her mother had said, she indeed had no heart? But she knew that wasn't so. She knew the depths of her feelings in other matters, if no one else did.

Three weeks after Pearl returned from her mother's funeral in Calgary, a moving van backed up the driveway and burly men unloaded the mahogany dining room suite, china barrels, wooden crates and boxes and carried them into the house. In the boxes were yellow and green, pink and blue satin-covered eiderdown quilts, Hudson's Bay blankets, linen tablecloths and serviettes. Inside the barrels and crates, packed in thin strips of newspaper and curls of wood shavings, were elegant glassware, china and silver serving dishes. Amy and Vivien were enlisted to unpack the set of pink roses Limoges china; the delicate German hot chocolate mugs; the silver teapot that had been a wedding gift to her parents from her father's family in Scotland.

With the money she inherited, Pearl took charge of the house. She added on a dining room to accommodate her parents' dining room suite, and a study for herself. Her new study, her *room of her own*, had a full wall of built-in bookshelves, one small window that looked into the forest and down the ravine, and a heavy padded door that she kept closed.

Pearl barged ferociously down her list. In the living room she replaced the red chaise longue and the overstuffed chairs with sleek Danish furniture. She ejected the old brass pole lamps with their creamy glass shades and trilights and replaced them with white origami-like fixtures suspended from the ceiling on long white cords. The Oriental magic carpets with their soft fringes vanished, and brown and green sisal the colour of algae and earth took their place and covered the hardwood floors wall to wall and down the hall to the second bathroom. Matching woven brown jute covered the walls. The bedrooms were redone. The driveway was paved, and a landscape architect consulted to plan gardens to flank the asphalt.

Her accomplishments made her proud, though no one seemed to appreciate the changes—the improvements—as much as she. Vivien wanted the "magic carpets," as she called them, back; Amethyst wanted the pole lamps of all things. Tom did not "care for" the sisal and would have liked to have been consulted. Pearl threw up her hands. Fine. She was through caring what people thought. She was getting things done. She was through waiting around for someone else to take action.

For several months, even a year, she seemed satisfied, almost happy for a while, reading in her room, pinning quotations up on the outside of her new study door:

Mother, wife, sweetheart are the jailers.
Or
Society, being codified by man, decrees that woman is inferior.
Or
All oppression creates a state of war.

After most of the money was gone and the house was, for the most part, how she wanted it, Pearl wasn't through yet. She lined up the daughters who remained at home and defiantly stared each of them in the face as she made her pronouncement: "I am finished being the victim. I am going to show you all what an intelligent, determined woman is capable of doing. I have learned that, I quote, *You cannot gain peace by avoiding life*, end quote, and I am finished avoiding *my* life. Look at me when I'm talking to you. I am no longer going to be dependent on your father for support that does not come. I am going to make my own money and do with my life as I please. I am going to become a teacher, and then the rest of you can bally well do as you like. I am finished caring. About you, and for you. I am going to have a life of my own, and you are not going to stop me."

Pearl submerged herself in her studies and came as close as she ever would to regaining the happiness she had felt at McGill. She went into her room and shut the door. How delicious! In addition to the textbooks required for her teaching certificate, Pearl began reading Bertrand Russell and George Sand. She taped new signs on her study door and changed them more often: *Few tasks are more like the torture of Sisyphus than housework, with its endless repetition; the clean becomes soiled, the soiled is made clean, over and over, day after day.*

She didn't stop caring for her family entirely, but she stopped setting the table for breakfast and left boxes of cereal, Pop-Tarts and a bowl of oranges on the counter. School lunches were Wagon Wheels, apples and Velveeta sandwiches. Instead of pot roast or chicken stew for supper, Pearl served them canned peas, canned corn, Minute Rice, Steakettes, fried Spam.

Tom came home after work and sat down at the table without speaking while his daughters passed him serving bowls and plates of food. When he stopped eating, he folded his serviette in half, then folded it again, and again. "I deserve better than this," he said quietly, excusing himself and rising from the table.

"Let me guess where you're going," said Pearl.

He said nothing.

Pearl got up, pushed her chair in. "Damn you all anyway," she said to her daughters. She went back into her study and closed the door. Then she opened it again. "And do the dishes."

Back and forth, back and forth, Pearl drove into Vancouver for night classes, and on weekends her study door was closed more than it was open. She immersed herself in the books, felt moments close to joy when her brain, reawakened, sucked up everything it could find.

Two semesters later, Pearl opened the manila envelope and with pride extracted her teaching certificate. Again she lined her daughters up in her study and told them with triumph in her voice, with something resembling happiness, and pride, that she was now qualified: she could find a job teaching high school English. She had truly broken her own shackles. She was an example to them all, she crowed, their father included. She did not need them, not any of them, and while they seemed incapable of much in the way of admiration, standing there so dumbly, Virginia Woolf would not have been. No longer would she be at their beck and call. They had better get used to not having her around, and that threat wasn't idle, either.

Pearl

Pearl sat on the bench of her boudoir table looking at her hair. She still had on her favourite flannelette pyjamas covered with little yellow flowers. Her black hair was shoulder-length now but still held its curl from the perm, and would bounce back into place when she brushed it, in a way that she liked. Today was her first job interview—the first of her life. She would look nice—professional and nice—for the interview. She was nervous, but she was well qualified, and well groomed, and the principal was a patient of Tom's. Which ought to work to her advantage, all things being fair. Her silver dressing set lay before her. She picked up her hairbrush to begin brushing her hair, counting the strokes to fifty. And as she did that, of course she thought about her sister May, as she always did when she brushed her hair, because May had always envied Pearl her dressing set because it was sterling silver while hers was only plate, because their parents hadn't approved of May's marriage. Every day Pearl brushed her hair and every day she thought of this. She swung around on the bench and bent over to brush her hair between her knees. Sides, ten each; front to back, ten; back to front, ten. She put her hairbrush down in its spot between the comb and the shoehorn, stood up, and unbuttoned her pyjama top. She took the top off and laid it on the bed and glanced at her partial nakedness in the mirror. At her loosening belly and fallen breasts with those large, dark nipples that had fed her four children. Those useless daughters of hers. What bliss an empty house. Next she pulled down her pyjama bottoms and stepped out of them and then picked them up. She folded her pyjamas neatly and put them under her pillow, patted the pillow, then smoothed the pillowcase. She crossed the room to her dresser, where she took out white cotton underpants and a white cotton brassiere. Next she pulled on her panty girdle. She sat down on the edge of the bed to unroll and put on her stockings, standing again to attach them to the garters as naturally as if she had done it a thousand times, and likely she had. Then she took a white dress slip from the drawer and slid it on over her head.

Pearl hadn't gone to May's wedding; they were living in Nanaimo at the time, because Tom was on a locum, and she had Ruby and Laurel to look after. May's wedding dress had been blue, of course. What other colour could May's wedding dress, or any other kind of dress of hers, possibly be? *Everything* always had to be blue. And why? To match her eyes, of course. Pearl slammed the underwear drawer shut. Why was she thinking all this today of all days? Blue this, blue that, blue the other thing, she said under her breath.

Nobody else could have blue. Why? Because until May came along, no one else in the family except their grandfather had blue eyes. And then, when May was born, lo and behold, she had blue eyes. Everyone in the family and down the block and around the corner was simply overjoyed, as one could imagine. From that moment on, she could do no wrong. It had made Pearl sick, and still did.

Why was she thinking about all that? She had better things to think about, like getting this job. Mad at herself now, Pearl slid open the tall closet doors and shoved the clothes on their hangers this way and that. She took out a black and white pleated skirt and put that on, next a white blouse with a wide pointed collar and handsome silver buttons up the front, and then finally she hiked up the skirt to pull the blouse down from underneath. She smoothed the skirt with her hands. She stood in her stockinged feet looking at herself in the full-length mirror. She would do. With some earrings and beads. She went to her jewellery box. Now, *it* was blue. Blue leather. How could *that* have happened?

Pearl put the earrings and beads down on the bathroom counter. She unzipped her makeup bag and took out her pancake makeup, rouge, powder and lipstick. She wet the sponge at the sink and applied the pancake, distorting her face as she did to tauten the flesh of her cheeks, chin, upper lip. She applied a tiny dab of rouge to each cheek and rubbed it in. Perhaps it was too much. She paused. Too late for that now. Next was the powder. Then she took a plastic-backed brush from the drawer and brushed her hair once again, though just a few strokes this time, and then she combed it into place. Next she took the can of VO5 out of the cupboard below the sink and she sprayed, generously coating her whole head of hair.

Pearl pulled the two outside mirror panels forward and inspected the back and sides of her hair. Wondered vaguely what she might be asked at the interview, about her teaching methods, which were formed very much from theory and not practice, and about her experience, which was pathetically little. Ah, well. She would find something to say. How one comported oneself was half the battle.

She was running out of time. Earrings. Beads. Ye gods, where were her shoes? She took her black pumps from the shoe rack. She stepped into the shoes and went again to stand in front of the full-length mirror.

She took her camel hair coat from the hall closet. Where were her gloves? Maybe she was nervous after all. She pulled on her gloves. She picked up her purse and walked to the front door. When she opened it, the horses whinnied at her over the fence. No one had fed them their oats this morning. Feed the animals first, her father always said, and so she put her purse in her car and went to the shed. Mr. Thompson would have to wait five minutes. What a difference riding horses had made to her childhood. She had loved to ride and had hoped her girls would too. But only Amethyst and Vivien appeared interested in the horses, and Amethyst was allergic. Laurel spent her time listening to her transistor radio and writing idiotic love poems in a notebook she kept under her mattress.

There was mud on her coat and she went back inside to sponge it off. Then she stood on the threshold before stepping back out of the house. This was it: she was going. In her garden the daffodils were out. The tulips were out. She pulled the front door closed behind her more firmly than she needed to, and she walked more quickly than she needed to, a tension in her body that implied escape, and climbed into her blue Ford Falcon and drove away.

Pearl's students were completely uninterested in anything she had to say and they would not be quiet. They threw things at each other and at her, and one day two boys made a fire in a garbage can in the aisle. She came home from that chaos to find the house a mess and there was no food to put on the table and everyone was mad at her for not being able to do it all and stared at her with sad faces. Ha! Her limbs had been tied to four horses and then someone had gleefully cried, "Gee haw!" Her life was all a huge disappointment and her resentment at the unfairness of it all grew. She felt like the pressure cooker, the safety bobbin tipping crazily on top as the trapped water screamed and threatened to blow. Ruby was gone and Laurel was gone and still there wasn't enough time in the day. She was late for everything. Supper was late and she was late for school. She was late dropping Amy and Vivien off at their lessons and she was late picking them up. It got worse, and she began to be ten, fifteen, twenty minutes late, half an hour, even an hour. Two. Then she was greeted by their sullen little faces. They didn't care what had happened to her, they didn't care how much she was trying to do, damn them, the selfish little wretches, as long as their needs were being met. Their supper. Their lessons. Their lunches. Sometimes she was held up so long by traffic or staff meetings or grocery shopping that she left them to their own devices. They could bally well walk home.

What was the matter, anyway? Life had become more, not less, difficult to manage. The money of her own to spend as she liked was most welcome, but at what cost to her? No one saw her struggle, or if they did, no one cared about her superhuman efforts on their behalf.

After all I've done for you. It was true, damn it all. She had driven them to their lessons. Taken them to the library, the art gallery, the beach. She had fed them. Washed them. Washed and ironed their clothes. Mended their clothes. They had always had books, and dogs, and then the horses—but nothing was ever enough. Their greed was insatiable, and not a single word of thanks ever crossed their lips.

Some days it was almost too much to bear. Some days she just let the floodgates open and abandoned any semblance of control, usually when her husband wasn't around, but on occasion when he was. You never saw a man disappear so fast. She knelt down and unleashed her rage, let loose crying, and wailing, lashing out at whoever came near. She screamed down the hall at the closed bedroom doors, *I am working all day and all night too, and for what? For what? What is the matter with you all?* She walked down the hall and struck out at their bedroom doors and at their bodies with her hands, with wooden spoons, and the yardstick. *Damn you!* She chased them. *Damn you all!* she shrieked, and she sobbed at their heartlessness, at how she had been abandoned, so unfairly, how she had always, *always* been unloved. Not one of them cared, nobody loved her. And then she got mad, and dried her tears, and called her children to her study. Soon enough, she warned, they would see just how little she cared. The children stared at the floor. They already knew.

On this, her second trip to Ireland, to Yeats country this time, she sat in a park in Sligo and stared long and hard at the place where two streams converged and became stronger. What a time she was having, away from all responsibility except to herself. How good it was to be completely free of encumbrances. To look after herself, only herself. She could sit here quietly forever, she thought, left alone, left to her solitude and her thoughts. And as she sat there, it came to her. Her older two daughters were for all intents and purposes gone. Amy was fourteen, Viv thirteen.

What was stopping her now? Not guilt for abandoning her children when they still needed her—they were all now in their teens or beyond. She had the means to support herself; she had a car, and her wits. She and Tom were sleeping in separate rooms now and barely spoke—they would not miss each other. She could leave. She could go.

But leave after sinking all that money into the house and property in her futile efforts to make it a home? It wasn't fair. But what choice was there? It was the price of her freedom. Either she accepted the cost or she paid more dearly—with the remainder of her life. She watched the water course by in front of her and thought fleetingly of Crane's ambivalent universe. Nothing, no one really cared. She would have to leave her study, her gardens, her origami light fixtures. Leave the place she had toiled over for almost twenty years. Where she had met failure day after day. Her determination not to give up, her stubborn stick-to-it-iveness had in the end been laughable, not laudable. She was as bad as her mother. And now, if anything was going to change, really change, it would have to be she, she who was the only one who took any initiative about anything, she who would have to leave if she was going to save herself, because she was the only one who gave a damn about her welfare. If she did not, she would be swallowed again by that world where she was never enough.

She had a choice. She did. She had thought about leaving before, had even tried to leave before, but her sense of responsibility had always brought her back, much notice anyone took of that. Maybe this time she would find the strength to put herself first. Maybe this time she could get it right. She mustn't rush. It might take another year to save her money and lay her plans, but now, now she saw a beacon of hope above the dark mess of things waiting for her at home. When she returned, she would not, she would *not* be swallowed up again by that family, that selfish, ungrateful family of hers.

Why was it so much easier to keep perspective, gain perspective, from a distance? She ought to know something about that from her art studies. In Ireland she could see what she needed to do, could see what was wrong, what was necessary to fix it. But back home, up to her neck in it again, she felt only in great danger, flailing, screaming, begging for sympathy that never came. No one loved her. No one cared. She had been a fool to think it might be otherwise. Hope after hope dashed on jagged rocks. No more. When she got back from her holiday, things were going to be different. She would play second fiddle no longer. She promised herself.

VIVIEN

Her bangs, usually cut short in a half moon, were shaggy and long, almost in her eyes. Barefoot, in cut-offs and a T-shirt, Viv, thirteen, was sitting on the mare, Dolly, out in the field, practising looking wistful, and practising whistling—both required holding her mouth in a particular way. Dolly had her head down, and was nibbling at the scanty remains of grass. She wasn't wearing a bridle; Viv had looped two hay ropes together and then noosed them loosely around the horse's muzzle. After a while she gave up on the whistling and began singing the songs she made up as she went along. Yearny cowboy songs. Songs based on the ones she heard on the radio at her friend Colleen's. *He don't love me, why don't he love me, please won't you love me.* Ballads of broken or breaking hearts.

She lay back on the horse's rump and looked up at the clouds. She had been so sure that turning thirteen would make a difference, but it hadn't. Who *was* she, anyhow? Someone named Vivien—Viv now, she had decided—who lived in that room and sat at that place at the table and whose name was on that drawer in the kitchen and above that coat hook in the playroom.

Someone who was going into grade nine in September. But what she *still* did not know, longed desperately to know, was what was the *matter* with her. What is *wrong* with you? her mother demanded again and again. What is the *matter* with you, Vivien?

She hadn't heard the questions for a while. Her mother was gone again. Not for good—she hadn't said that for a while—but on a holiday, one of the holidays the money from her teaching job allowed her to take now. This time she was far, far away in Ireland, and right then, in that moment, Vivien was feeling good. She loved being on Dolly. She liked the feel of the old mare under her, her warm fur and regular breathing. Viv's legs and cut-offs were filthy because Dolly hadn't been brushed or curry-combed in a long time, and her dusty fur came off in drifts and handfuls, and stuck to Viv's clothes and her legs. Viv didn't care about the dirt, but when she went back to the house she'd have to shuck her clothes at the back door and run naked to her room so that Amy wouldn't get allergic.

She had thought she'd be with Amy today, that Amy would take her allergy pill and catch the horses with her, that the two of them would ride bareback out of the field and down the driveway, through the gardens and past their low blue house. They would follow the path through the trees and down into the ravine to the creek near the woods. While the horses stood up to their knees in the cool running water and yanked tall, lush grass from the banks, green slobber drooling from their mouths, she and Amy would have lain back along the horses' spines and watched the sky and the clouds and talked about movie stars and singers and measured to see whether Amy's hair was long enough yet to touch her bra strap if she tilted her head way back. Or maybe they would have stayed up in the orchard, and while they sat on the corral fence rails eating golden plums the horses would pull apples from the trees. But instead she was by herself, because Amy had gone shopping for slingbacks with Jeanette.

Dolly, fifteen hands high, stood perfectly still except for the occasional quiver to rid herself of a fly. Her head was held low, her eyes were half closed as she dozed. Viv sat up, felt tall. She liked the view of the world from here, she liked being on Dolly bareback; liked the pleasant discomfort of the horse's spine hard against her coccyx.

This morning in the corral, Dolly's colt had come up behind Viv, breathed his warm horse breath on her neck, waggled his big ears, nibbled her ear with his big fleshy lips. She had been mean to him. "No," she had said, and shoved his head away. "Go away. I don't want you." When he didn't move, she pushed on his chest, trying to force him to move back. Stubbornly, he set his hooves and wouldn't budge. "Get out of here, I said!" She had turned her back on him and moved several feet away. He followed her. Lightly pushed her in the back with his head. She smiled, turned, murmured love words, called him her dear one, and kissed the place where his shoulder met his neck, kissed the sides of his velvet muzzle, his soft reddish-brown and white nose, put her arms around his strong, smooth neck.

Sometimes she thought about her mother when she was alone like this. In some vague sort of way she still hoped that she might start to like her. That maybe when Pearl got back from Ireland she would be happier, and nicer, and stay that way this time. And that by some magic she, Viv herself, would have changed too, and that her mother would finally be able to love her. Viv closed her eyes and felt them fill with tears. Before she had left for the airport, Pearl had screamed at her. It was nothing new, but Viv wasn't ready for the attack, hadn't had a chance to brace herself. As Pearl approached her, she had thought she was maybe going to kiss her goodbye, maybe say something nice because she was going away for so long. When her mother had come towards her, Viv had even offered a little smile. She hadn't really looked at her mother; if she had, she would have known. Pearl told her to shut her trap and listen even though she hadn't said a word. Then she'd said she couldn't stand the sight of Viv one second longer and would be glad to be rid of her. And then she had left. Just left, and Vivien had stood there for a long time and then she had gone down to the woods, to her own little nook in the trees, and curled up against the thick, deep roots.

Now, lost in memory, she lost her balance, slipped off the horse's back and fell to the ground with a thump. She didn't move; she lay on her back on the stony earth and looked up at Dolly beside her. At Dolly's brown and white legs, and furry belly. The old mare slowly swung her head around. She met Viv's gaze with her big brown eyes. She reached over and breathed her warm breath on the girl's face. Viv looked at Dolly's soft brown muzzle and the yellow and green slobber and smelled her grassy breath. The mare gently nuzzled her, and Viv looked into the horse's kind eyes, and beyond, up at the sky, and felt the world, the earth, hard under her.

Around Easter the following spring, Amy confided to Viv as they smoked out her bedroom window that she liked Rusty, the oldest cousin of the Gagliardi kids across the street. She liked his red hair, she said; she liked how he was always laughing and being a smartass and getting into trouble; she liked how he didn't care about anything, and she didn't care that he wasn't that smart. Her private-school friends wouldn't think much of him, but she didn't really care, she said. So what?

Rusty had dropped out of high school. He was sixteen now, working nights catching chickens and turkeys and loading them onto trucks. He had deep, ugly scratches on his arms from the birds as they tried to escape the blinding lights and cruel hands that grabbed them. When he got paid, Rusty hung around outside the beer parlour of the Beresford Arms or outside the liquor store by the Dairy Queen looking for someone to buy him a bottle, or a case of beer. If he wasn't there, he'd succeeded, and was off partying with Barry, his best friend, if he'd talked him into skipping school.

Sometimes Rusty brought Barry over to the Gagliardis' and Viv, sitting concealed in the hawthorn tree at the end of her driveway, looked over and watched him longingly, living her lovesick cowboy songs as Barry put his cigarette in his mouth while he combed his straight, strawberry blond hair forward and then flicked it back out of his small blue eyes with a toss of his head. That toss was so cool she thought she'd die each time he reached into the back pocket of his skin-tight jeans for the broken rat-tail comb.

That summer she turned fourteen, after Pearl had flown to England to visit the Lake District. Ruby was still in California, finished college, working at the Sierra Club. Laurel was a clerk at the Bay in Victoria and dating a guy who had picked her up hitchhiking. Amethyst was on the French Riviera for the summer practising her French. Tom was in Ontario with his sisters. So Viv was left at home with the two dogs, a freezer full of frozen pizzas, a cupboard full of canned lasagna, spaghetti, wieners and beans, and a standing order with the milkman.

Viv threw herself a birthday party the day after the last of her family left. Deep Purple and the Stones blasted out from Tom's big Heathkit speakers; so did Jethro Tull, Alice Cooper, Janis Joplin, Canned Heat, Uriah Heep and The Doors. Hour after hour, day and night, the music pounded, vibrating the windows and making the dogs howl to go outside. The fridge was jammed with beer and Coke and Tang; bottles of rye and vodka stood beside empty ice-cube trays in sticky puddles on the counters. The floors were dirty and sticky, the ashtrays and garbage overflowing, while up and down the driveway Viv's guests—Rusty and Barry and their friends—came and went. As they partied into the morning, Viv told them to crash in any of the bedrooms, cover themselves with the Hudson's Bay blankets and the green and yellow, and blue and pink satin duvets that had come from her grandparents' house. They drank from the Frenchwoman's crystal glasses, they wiped up spills with embroidered tea towels and hand-tatted doilies.

It took a lot of standing near him, smiling at him, asking him for lights for her smokes, for a sip of his drink, but finally Barry offered to get Viv a beer, which she didn't want but drank because she would have drunk anything he brought her, and an hour or two later he offered her one of his smokes and lit it in his mouth before he handed it over. Their fingers touched. She was transported. Later that night, alone, almost overcome with joy, she stood in front of Pearl's dressing table mirror and lifted her shirt to see the little breasts budding on her chest. Their timing was perfect.

Things were different when Pearl got back from England. She didn't comment anymore on where Viv was or what she did, whereas before she had been at her constantly. Viv, too, was different. She had a boyfriend. She'd had sex. So she didn't ask permission for anything, either; she did whatever she wanted, and nothing happened. She went out on school nights, and Barry picked her up after school if she hadn't already skipped. Her mother never spoke to her directly, just maintained this hostile silence, glared at her, or through her, if she caught her eye, left her notes on the blackboard she installed next to the back door. *Take out the garbage. Make your bed.* She was only slightly nicer if Amy came home for the weekend. She was like walking anger, Viv thought. Walking, talking, breathing, and Viv, alone with her more than anyone else, was afraid of her, and uneasy, especially at night.

Pearl had moved into Laurel's old bedroom when she returned from overseas, next door to Viv's, and the wall was thin, plywood, and Viv lay in her own bed listening to her mother's sobs and wailing, hating her, wishing she would shut up, would go away again, this time forever, if she didn't like them so much, would just leave them alone. If they all made her so goddam miserable, then why the hell didn't she just *go*? It seemed like every night she was crying and yelling, Viv told Barry. Her father didn't hear, or he didn't say anything, and why should he either if she had moved out of their bedroom and treated him like shit. No wonder he was never home. How many calls could there be? How many operations to perform? How many rounds to do? It was like she wanted Viv to hear her, she said, so that someone—Viv herself, she supposed, since she was the only one around—would take pity on her and do something. Why would she, though, even if she could? They hated each other. And her mother smelled, too, though she didn't tell Barry that. She smelled all strange and bloody. There were gross sanitary pads in the bathroom garbage, and big bags of Kotex in the cupboards. Everything about her mother was repulsive, disgusting.

She and Barry—her darling Bear—spent their days driving around in his car until they ran out of money for gas and went back to his place to bum off his mother. Player's Filter on the dash and a beer or a paper cup of rye and Coke between his legs, and a magnum bottle of sparkling wine between hers, Viv told Bear that she liked how his crotch looked when he drove; when he took the beer from between his legs with his hangnailed fingers; when he put it back between his legs. She liked how his crotch looked with the hard-on she gave him by stroking him through his jeans.

A dozen times a night they joined the parade of other cool Beresford people in their cool cars, their Super Bees, jacked-up '57 Chevs, Challengers, Novas, Mustangs, driving the main street from one end of Beresford to the other between the A&W and the Dog 'N Suds. And like the other cool people, they reversed into the back of the lot, turned on their lights and waited for the carhop. Hi-Boy burgers with cheese, Coney fries, root beer. When she was with Barry, she felt good: *finally* she was loved. He'd promised it'd be forever. And now she had stuff to tell Amy when she came home on weekends, instead of the other way around. She rested her hand lightly on the inside of Barry's thigh.

"I love you, Bear," she said.

"I love you, Baby Round Eyes," he said.

Viv lit two smokes. "Here," she said, passing him one. Moved her hand back to his crotch and stroked him. Then she removed her hand and made smoke rings. "Suffer, baby, suffer," she said, laughing at his pleading eyes. "That's all you get today." Later, though, she might change her mind. Sex was okay, though not as good as what she had thought it would be. She liked the thump-thump of their hearts as they lay naked against one another, their bodies joined. The feel of his chest and belly against hers. His surrender as he came. So after he had pleaded enough, she usually let him in. Why not? She burrowed her head under his arm; she wanted to be close, close to him, to climb right inside him.

Over at Barry's in front of the colour TV, or at the parties his parents threw in their rec room, and in the Legion halls and community halls during dances where his brother's band played—Barry played the drums—Viv learned to chain-smoke, and to guzzle, puke and pass out on rye and Coke, and vodka and Tang, and Andrés Pink Perle. She wore a curly dark brown wig and piled on the makeup so she looked old enough to drink, and she sat at the band table smoking and drinking with the other wives and girlfriends. When the dance was over and the band was packing up, she went around to the long tables with their newsprint tablecloths and picked up drinks people had left and drank them. Barry, who never picked a fight, told her it was a stupid thing to do, told her to stop, but by then she was too drunk to care. She *loved* being drunk—she *loved* not giving a *fuck* and then passing out, she loved being *gone*. The world stopped, and someone who loved her looked after her. And if he was really hammered, Barry would even carry her, his drunken Juliet, all the way into her house and her bedroom. He'd lay her down on her bed and cover her up with her quilt before he ran back down the driveway to his car.

October passed and neither of her parents had said a word about anything she did. Maybe they didn't even notice when she stopped coming home at all because she had moved in with Barry and his parents. So fuck it, she said.

Life at Barry's was simple and close and exactly what it appeared to be. No charged silences, no poison darts, no having to guess what everything meant beneath its surface the times when it wasn't smack in your face. No angry words that stayed hovering like pollution in anger-filled air. No one yelled. They ate borscht made by his father, and Kraft Dinner, and cabbage rolls, and toast. Viv slept in Barry's bedroom and he slept on the couch until his parents went to bed and then he came in and sometimes they had sex and talked about what they'd do when they were married.

Viv went to school some days and some days she just lay around the house watching TV and smoking cigarettes until Barry, who had quit school, got home from working at his dad's gas station. His parents spent nights in the beer parlour of the Beresford Arms or the Legion. Before paydays, when they were broke, they holed up in the TV room with Barry and Viv, sipping beer or instant coffee. Now *this* was a family, she thought, safe and warm between Barry and his mother, bumming smokes off his dad, watching TV movies. *This* was a family who did stuff together.

Still, just before Christmas she wanted to go home, and lying in her own bed listening to the heavy silence in the house, she noticed how particularly hostile it was this year. And how empty the house was, except for the dogs. Ruby was staying in California with her fiancé, a fellow who owned a car wash. Laurel was banned for setting a bad example because she was now living in sin with the hitchhiking guy. But at least Amy came home, and the two sisters hung out their bedroom windows like old times.

As Christmas Day approached, the tension ratcheted up in a familiar, almost reassuring way, with Pearl's usual complaints about having to do everything herself and how she was going to leave and then see how they all liked that. But no one cared about her anymore. "The family tradition," said Amy under her breath. "Right on track."

If he was home, Tom practised playing Christmas carols for a choral concert and the joyful tunes clashed with the atmosphere of doom. Doors in the house were closed. The newest sign on Pearl's study door read: *Man can will nothing unless he first understands that he must count on no one but himself; that he is alone, abandoned on earth in the midst of his infinite responsibilities, without help, with no other aim than the one he sets himself, with no other destiny than that one he forges for himself on this earth.*

Two days before Christmas, Amy and Vivien watched their mother as she called the dogs and they jumped happily into her car. They watched as she lugged her suitcases out of the house, put the largest piece in the trunk at the front of the car and dropped the hood. They watched as she pulled on her gloves and climbed into the car, closed the door firmly, checked her lipstick in the rear-view mirror. She ignored them completely. She started the car, put it in reverse, backed into the turnaround, drove down the driveway and disappeared into her future. She didn't wave goodbye and neither did they. When the car turned out of the driveway, Amy looked at Viv. They lifted their eyebrows and gave each other a tentative smile. Viv took the deck of smokes out of the front of her jeans and they lit cigarettes out in the open.

"The taste of freedom," said Viv.

"Tastes good," said Amy.

They expected that she would call within a few hours, and she did. Other times Amy had said what she was supposed to say and their mother had come back. But this time it was Viv who answered the phone. She held out the receiver to Amy, but Amy wouldn't take it. Viv hung the phone back up and that was the end of that.

Viv hopped in and took her place beside Barry on the console between the bucket seats and took the smoke he had lit for her. "Thanks, Bear," she said. Then, along with six cases of beer and three magnums of Pink Perle, bags of chips and a few tabs of organic mescaline, Barry, Gary, Colleen, Larry, Marlene, John and Viv all took off in Gary's Mustang and Barry's Dodge. Larry opened beer bottles with his teeth and passed the bottles between the cars as they pulled alongside each other. Bear popped the plastic cork from a bottle of Pink Perle against the roof of the car while Viv held the steering wheel, and Marlene lit a joint. Yahoo! No, Viv had told her father, she couldn't go to Banff for the May long weekend because she was going camping with Brenda and Laurie from CGIT. Amy had told him she had to study for her finals.

They got off on the mescaline just as they arrived at their campsite, a meadow near a stream at the end of a grassy lane. They started laughing as they put the tents up in grass that had become *unbelievably* green and lush, in wildflowers that were *unbelievably* abundant, and beautiful beyond description. Everything in the world was now vibrant, enhanced, lovely. How mind-blowing fucking fantastic it was to be alive! They ripped open bags of ripple chips and boxes of Bugles. Barry blew up the empty chip bags and popped them and they laughed and drank and smoked some more. Finally everyone else wandered off down the trails and into the woods, and Barry and Viv stripped naked and lay down in the sun together on their sleeping bags.

Amy came right out of the house when Viv got home. "You aren't going to believe this," she said. On Saturday morning a moving van had backed slowly up their driveway. The men in coveralls presented a long list written in Pearl's careful, controlled hand. Amy hadn't known whether to help them find the things Pearl had listed or not. She knew she'd get in trouble if she did, and anyway she didn't want to help her mother steal things from their home. But she'd get into worse trouble from Pearl if she didn't. She wouldn't get to wear the red velvet opera cape with the ermine collar that Pearl had worn to parties and balls at McGill to her own high school graduation. And Pearl had bought her the most beautiful graduation dress, with chiffon sleeves, an empire waist and tiny roses running beneath the bust. And she had bought her a car. And Amy had been promised a trip to the hairdresser's where her long, thick, wavy hair would be done in big looped curls with pale yellow satin ribbons running through them. Amy had helped the moving men, and the house echoed when they went in the front door.

It was Laurel who told Tom on the phone, from Victoria, that Viv was pregnant. That night he came into her bedroom and she kept her eyes on the floor, on the white linoleum with gold streaks running through it. Her old sock doll, Stuffy, was in her arms, and she was curled up on her side. Her father stood silently beside her bed—her bed where, when she was a little girl, he had checked her stomach for gastrointestinal upset, where he had put his hand on her forehead to check for fever. What was the matter with her now? What *was* she now? Child, or woman?

"Vivien?"

"Yes, Daddy?" She focused on her curtains and matching blue quilt with the big white and yellow daisies.

"Are you awake?"

"Yes."

He sat down on the edge of her bed. "What are we going to do about you?"

"I don't know."

"Do you want to get married?"

"No."

"Well," he said, "that's one good thing." There was a long silence and then he kissed her on the forehead and left. She heard him repeat it as he walked down the empty hall, and down the stairs into the empty living room, and up the other side into the empty dining room. *Well, that's* one *good thing.* She heard him fixing himself a drink, and then another a short while later. And another. *That's* one *good thing, now, isn't it?*

Pearl came to the United Church home in Burnaby just once, right before she left on her extended trip to Portugal. Viv didn't want to see her, didn't want her to come, wanted to be left alone. You have a visitor, Mrs. Lansdowne had said, without telling her who it was. It didn't occur to her that it might be her mother until she saw her gloves on the chair inside the door. They had met in a small consultation room, were in closer proximity than they had been in years. Pearl was businesslike and matter-of-fact. She said that she didn't have much time, but she felt it was important for her to come and see Vivien. She felt it was her duty to counsel abortion. It was legal now. She did not try to touch her daughter. Viv braced her body and her mind and stared stonily at the floor, did not look at her mother, did not answer her. Pearl stood up, pulled on her gloves and left. "I hate you," Viv whispered at the door.

Through the long months of the pregnancy, she distanced herself from her body as it changed, and she became so removed she barely saw it growing, barely felt and did not acknowledge the baby forming and moving inside her. She lay on her bed in her room thinking, thinking, staring out the window, reading

Agatha Christie, smoking, waiting for Barry to come and pick her up and take her out of here, out of this place, take her home to his place. She avoided herself, her body, until all those months later labour began and she was jolted violently back into herself as the assault on her began, as the baby demanded to be born.

She had never held a baby before she held him, fresh from her body, handed him by a young nurse who hadn't known not to bring her baby to her. She was amazed and mystified as she held him in her arms for those few minutes. That terrifying, blinding, red and black pain and now this baby. This *baby.* And what happened next? What was going to happen to her next? He made her afraid. She didn't want to be a mother. She couldn't be a mother. What did she know about babies or having babies? Nothing. What did she know about herself? Nothing. He had to be given up, she told Barry. He had to be given away to parents who wanted a baby, were ready for a baby.

She began dressing to leave the hospital, and as she took off the green gown she moved gingerly, her lower parts still sore and loose. Her fleshy belly felt like porridge. Her breasts, aching, were bound. She wanted to go home. Only that: to go home. But she couldn't get on her clothes. Her shirt wouldn't button. She couldn't get on her jeans. What was wrong? What had happened? How could she not be how she thought she was?

Vancouver B.C.
April 1973
Dear Vivien,

I am not going to mince words with you. What an absolute monster you have been. Don't tell me you didn't cook up all that rotten scene with the pregnancy on purpose, to twist the knife just as cruelly as you could. The fact that you caused your own self to suffer as well just happened. You weren't thinking, or simply didn't know ahead of time, that Life occasionally deals out a little retributive justice.

Dear heaven. That I gave so much thought to child-rearing and education, and yet still produced four such worthless human beings. What oh what has become of motherhood, that I could try to make something of it, something really great, and end up in a basement room too tired to prepare a decent meal for myself. To heck with the crew of you. It's all out for myself from here on, and any regard from me to you will be earned by you.

Yours, your once-loving mother.

P.S. I'm slowly making my way, once again, through David Copperfield. *I can't believe such cruelty to children. It seems to me you four had such an idyllic childhood. It did not prepare you for life.*

The log cabin was five miles from the Radium Hot Springs junction, nestled in the woods at the end of a dirt lane. She had hitchhiked across the province, having asked Barry to take her to the highway, to leave her there with her duffle bag, and unhappily he did. Phone me, he said. Call me collect, he said. But she didn't. She wanted as far away from her life as she could get, and she wasn't going back. Ever.

Inside the cabin there was a wooden kitchen table, two chairs and a stool, futon couch, wood stove, cupboards with spoons for handles, and a sleeping loft upstairs. Everything painted powder blue. The cold running water came from a stream behind the cabin.

Viv worked nights in the lounge of the hotel where the trucker had let her out, at the junction of the highways. Seemed as good a place as any to try to find work, and she did, taking that as a sign. She learned on the job to make highballs, tequila sunrises, dirty mothers, worked up to the fizzes, sours, margaritas. And Scotch with one ice cube, no mix. Viv's new man, Paul Hancock, drank the Scotch, when he could afford it. Double shots of Johnny Walker Red, or Chivas.

He called her "V" and she thought he was a god the way he handled her body and made her come. He knew her better than anyone ever had. After two weeks of dating—of fucking, and drinking—he had parked his dented black truck in front of the cabin, and dumped his tools and clothes in a big heap on the painted kitchen floor, where they stayed until she shoved them under the table. Paul was an older man—twenty-seven—and short and strong and fat, with sharp blue eyes that penetrated her being and thrilled her. He took charge of her. And look what he'd done for her with that tongue and those fingers. "You like that, V, don't you?" he whispered. "Answer me. Don't you, V?"

For her nineteenth birthday, he gave her a tab of acid and the promise of a bottle of wine he'd have to borrow her car to go into town to buy because his truck was running on fumes. Be right back, he said, and she stayed outside in the warm night until she started getting off and then she went back inside the cabin and sat on a kitchen chair. At first it was fun, laughing her head off, watching everything that began to move, watching the fabulous living beadwork adorning the cupboard doors making and remaking itself in exquisite patterns, and staring at the light blue log walls of the cabin, watching them thicken and thin as they breathed with her, in and out.

She glanced over to the brick-and-board bookshelf and saw the present her mother had sent from Ecuador. She was teaching at some college in Quito. Good riddance. Good absence. Viv tried to eye the gift, still wrapped, neutrally, but she was suspicious. What nasty surprise might it contain? She stared at the package for a long while before she decided to try to open it. Would it make her bigger, or smaller, this present? She figured out how to get her fingers to undo the pale pink ribbon—real ribbon, all satiny-soft and smooth—and she lifted the lid from a small cardboard box. Inside, wrapped in white tissue paper, were two antique cameo brooches. The larger one had the profile of a Greek goddess on it, a goddess whose skin was pure white against the light brown of the shell, her hair abundant and finely carved, a half-moon crown on her head, the cameo itself framed in plain pinkish gold. The profile on the smaller one was less ornate, the Victorian woman's skin creamy, the shell pinky, and the frame was not gold. Before she could make her fracturing mind think clearly, Viv loved them both. One in each of her fists, she warmed their cool shell faces and their hard metal edges. Then she put them down on the table and opened the envelope and the little flowered card. Her mother had written in her neat and careful handwriting that the cameos had belonged to Gramma Opal, and now they were to be Viv's. "With love from your mother on your nineteenth birthday."

Love from your mother. Viv hesitated, couldn't form thoughts. Love? From her mother? She needed to be careful. Why *really* was her mother giving her these? Her mind did a starburst and she couldn't figure it out. She began thinking about her Gramma Opal and how these had been hers, and a kaleidoscope of memories followed. Her grandmother hugging her as they sat together on the bed in their flannelette nighties. Gramma Opal taking out her hairpins, her long braids falling down her back like ropes. Vivien helping her unplait her braids and watching the tresses slither off her grandmother's shoulders the way trouble ought to, too. Viv wrapped her arms around herself, rocked gently. She could have stayed in her grandmother's arms forever. (All her life this craving to be held, just held.) And now Gramma Opal was dead, had been dead a long time, and she had died alone, and lonely, with no one to hold her, and Viv had not thought about her until now. She began to weep, then sob with sorrow, with remorse, and then, briefly, for herself and her own loneliness.

Time passed and she managed to pin the smaller brooch on the collar of her jean jacket, even though it kept melting. She wore the jacket with the cameo for the rest of the night as she sat by the window on the wooden-runged chair, waiting for Paul to come back. As the rainy dawn came, she finished coming down, endured the stark, ugly, depressing part of the acid stone. Paul hadn't come back.

O Life. How quickly she became the woman in a hurtin' song like the ones she had sung as a kid wandering up and down the driveway. Hopeless and helpless—that was her, all right. *Ow–ow-owwwwwww* howled the coyotes to the vast and glittering dark sky, *ow-owww* she howled when Paul hit her. His slaps and shoves became punches and kicks. Twenty, twenty-one, twenty-two, and one thing she had learned since moving to the Valley was about karma, and karma was about getting what you deserved, and she didn't need to be told that this was payback time for treating Barry so badly. For dumping him and buggering off. She deserved this.

At least she knew where Paul was when he left her in the truck listening to eight-track tapes of Fleetwood Mac and the Eagles. He was inside a cabin on the lake, or a chalet at the ski hill, talking to people about renos. He'd make them a deck, pour concrete, build a fence, a kennel for their dog, make a stained glass lamp for their dining room table. Anything that paid he said he could do, and then figured out how to do it.

He'd let her come along for the ride and then tell her to be a good girl and "Sit. Stay," which he thought was so funny. He slammed the truck door and left her, would forget about her for hours. "Hey, leave me some smokes," she said, and he tossed half a deck of Player's Plain at her through the open window. She wondered if the people inside knew she was out there and, if they did, what they thought of that, what he had told them. She wrapped herself in an old quilt and woke up freezing when Paul staggered out into the grey dawn still half pissed and hung over.

She was lucky if he got drunk and passed out somewhere else, or if he drank so fast he passed out before something pissed him off and he came after her. Some nights he pinned her on the bed with his strong, fat body and took his fat hand and pushed the fleshy heel of his palm against her nose as if he were going to crush it flat to her head, his fat fingers pressing hard against her cheekbones. In the dark of night, curled against his fat back, often drunk herself, she wondered why she stayed. Why did it feel right to be treated like shit? Why did she find some weird sort of comfort in it? At first it had been so exciting. That she—she!—was able to evoke such a powerful response.

Now she was lying hungover in their bed feeling like hell. She dropped her cigarette into a Heineken bottle. She didn't like Rothman's; they tasted crappy. But she had run out of Player's last night and Gordine had given her these. She could hear Paul grunting in the bathroom. The pig. She reached over to turn the radio up. The stretch made her wince. He had got her a good one last night. They were drinking beer at the end, and Paul didn't like beer. She didn't like beer either, but like the cigarettes, there wasn't anything else so she drank it. That's what you do. You make do with what you've got. Adapt or die. When the bar closed and she wouldn't steal him a bottle of Scotch, he got pissed off. And then it was the same old story. Except perhaps worse than usual.

There was the letter that had come from her mother. The letter asking if she was going to work in a bar all her life. Asking her if she knew where her life was headed. As if her mother had a clue about anything to do with her. Was Vivien truly going to waste her good brain, her opportunities, every chance she had been given? What was the matter with her? What did she want from life? I wash my hands of you, she had said in closing. Thank God, Viv had said.

She had burned the letter—good riddance to bad rubbish—but over the next few nights the questions had remained as she delivered the trays of drinks and clean ashtrays to tables, brought back empty glasses and bottles, full ashtrays, soiled cocktail napkins, broken stir sticks, cherry stems, orange and lemon rinds, and coins. Tips. As she washed the ashtrays, loaded the dishwasher, filled the cardboard beer cases with empties and stacked them in the back room.

Last night, when she was still working, she'd left the lounge for a pee and, sitting on the toilet, she'd started thinking about how Paul was always there waiting for her at the bar, usually sipping the Scotch she had to buy him with her tips. After the months, no, the years of this, where *was* she going? She had rested her elbows on her thighs and lowered her head onto her hands and watched the water turn yellow. She was sick of it all. Paul didn't know what he was doing any more than she did. He wasn't heading goddam anywhere and neither was she.

She lit another smoke and lay back in bed. University. Took another drag. Her lungs ached. One cigarette after another. One drink after another. She'd started sneaking a Kahlúa cow before work. A Caesar or two during. A Spanish coffee after. Sneaking. Stealing. More bad karma. She never laughed anymore. She never smiled. There was a university in Calgary, three hours away.

She had wanted to be the kind of person who didn't quit, who stuck with things even when they got difficult. Who did not choose a sheltered life over an unsheltered one. She wanted real life. She touched her ribs. A bit too real. So when was that karmic debt she owed to Barry paid, anyway? How much was enough, and how was she supposed to tell? And what were you supposed to do if the end of your life was looking a lot closer than what you actually had in mind? Paul was getting worse.

Bruises, broken ribs, broken nose, black eyes. What kind of love was that?

"You're very late, Vivien."

"Hi, Mum." Viv squashed her cigarette out in the ashtray and angrily exhaled. Already her mother was being a bitch. Great. Viv pulled the cuffs on her shirt down over her wrists. She opened the car door and got out, pulling down her shirt and sucking in her gut while saying under her breath, "The five fucking minutes that would have changed the world."

"You may as well come in," her mother said, turning towards her house. "You're looking much bigger. Are you getting fat?"

"Thanks," Viv said, gingerly opening the trunk and lifting out her suitcase.

Her mother stopped, turned and took two steps towards her. For a mindless split second Viv thought she was going to open her arms. Viv stopped breathing.

"Did you hear what I said?" Pearl said. "I *said*, are you getting fat?"

"Yes. Yes, I am. Are you?" Viv pushed past her mother and up the back steps into the house as rudely as she could. Pulled her bag like it was her life through the laundry room and kitchen and down the hall to the spare bedroom, directly across from her mother's. No lock on the door. She closed it. Leaned up against it like they did in movies. Already asking herself why in hell she was here. What was it that she was hoping would happen when she visited her mother? Rebirth? She laid her suitcase down in front of the door, rammed it in close and opened it. Took out the mickey. Unscrewed the lid and took a belt. Vodka for the faint of heart. Her whole body on red alert.

In the living room, her mother was sitting in her brown chair under the only light, a pole lamp, holding her knitting bag on her lap. "Sit over there," she said, indicating the couch. "I always sit here, in my special chair."

"I know," Viv said. "All right."

"Your towels are in the bathroom on the counter. Don't use mine."

Only a small amount of light filtered in through the filthy, big picture window. A giant Douglas fir loomed over the house, and the ground directly outside was laden heavily with dry, fallen needles; the lawn was dead. Heavy of heart, Viv turned back to the room and pushed her hand back and forth across the nub of the couch's grubby blue and beige flowers.

"You could try that tomato juice diet," Pearl said. "Do you remember what your father did with Bill the Garbageman's wife? *She* was too fat. Your father put her in the hospital and allowed her only tomato juice for ten days." She paused. "Your father had no use for fat women." Then she gave Viv one of her looks. Viv dropped her eyes. "He never encouraged me to make pies and cakes. Not that I could have made them anyway. 'We can do without that sort of thing,' he said. *His* mother, by the way, had a weight problem much of her life. My mother became fat as well. But *I* am not fat and never have been." She glared at her daughter. "Surely that's *something* in my favour." Pearl leaned forward and passed Viv a plate of Dad's cookies. "Will you have a cookie?"

"Thank you."

"It's very warm weather for a long-sleeved shirt. Do you have to keep doing that?"

"Doing what?"

"Fidgeting. Moving your hands back and forth like that across the fabric of the chesterfield. It's annoying."

"Sorry."

"You may pour the tea, if you can manage without spilling. I'll take mine clear."

"Sure." Viv leaned forward and tipped a dead fly out of her cup and onto the rug.

"What did you just do?"

"Nothing."

"You did something."

"No. I didn't." Viv poured the tea and spilled. Fuck.

"Pass me the sugar and lemon. You'll have to get a cloth from the kitchen to mop that up."

"I'd figured that out, believe it or not."

The sugar was hard in the bowl and had to be scraped out. The lemon slices were attractively arranged, but the lemon itself was old and mushy.

"Where are the cookies?" Pearl said.

"What cookies?"

"The *cookies.* Have you eaten them all?"

Shit. Where were they? The plate was empty. Next she'd eat the couch.

"Yes."

"Well, aren't you the selfish thing."

"Yes."

"Vivien, I've already had just about enough of you and you've barely been here an hour. Your behaviour casts a pall over everything. I think you go out of your way to be unpleasant. I really do."

Viv glared back at her mother. Then she said, "You read me like a book, Mum. Always have." Then she laced her hands together in her lap and bounced up and down like an idiot. "I do go out of my way to be unpleasant." She stopped bouncing and looked directly at her mother's knitting bag. The long green needles with the brown ends were sticking out. She breathed in and raised her eyes to her mother's. They hardened. "And I *am* fat, selfish and unpleasant. What *you* may not know, because you know almost nothing about me—is that I also drink too much." Viv stopped, surprised. She'd never said that before.

"Pooh," Pearl said. "I'm sure you don't."

Viv clenched her jaw. How the hell would she know?

"You never believe me. You never have. You have never believed *in* me, either. But do you know what I think? What I *really* think? That it would be better for everyone if I were dead. I don't know why I don't kill myself and put everyone out of their misery." Viv stared hard at Pearl. Hated it that she was going to whine. "Do you? Mum?"

Pearl laughed. "You always did have a flair for the dramatic, Vivien. Now get up off that substantial posterior of yours and go out to the kitchen and get some Kleenex and more cookies. I'd like one now, and I don't mind if you have another. One cookie more or less won't make the difference between heaven and hell, now, will it? Then I'd like to take you out for dinner, to celebrate your degree."

While Pearl dressed, Viv took a Perrier from the refrigerator and filled a tall glass with ice. Her degree, yes. Her degree. She drank deeply. Why did she even give a fuck about what her mother thought? About anything? She didn't. She didn't fucking care. She carried the half-empty glass down the hall to her bedroom and gave it a serious spike. As she left the room, she toasted the pictures of Amethyst on the dresser and walls. Amy in that pretty white formal with the tiny pink roses under the bust and her hair done in loops and satin ribbons for her high school graduation. Amy in mortar and gown graduating from a *good* university when she was twenty-one. Amy in white lace for her wedding. Viv held out her drink and rattled the ice. "To good girls," she said.

She took her drink and went back down the hall, through the kitchen and outside onto the patio. Night was falling, but the air was still warm. She sat down on the white plastic chaise longue. Her stomach was gurgling, the ice-cold liquid swishing around in her empty belly. It was past seven and she was starving. But she could wait. She was good at waiting, as long as she had a drink and a smoke. Hadn't she got good at waiting thanks to her mother? Good at something. All those times she and Amy had waited and waited for her to come and get them. They had always arrived late for their lessons and then she was late picking them up, sometimes by more than an hour. And sometimes she never showed up at all. If it wasn't too far, they walked. If not, they just sat there—what else could they do? They sat on the steps of their piano teacher's house peering at the road. They sat at the dinner table with the ballet teacher's family. They stood at the minister's living room window looking out, praying God please God please make her hurry up. Only to each other, in their looks more than in words, had they asked where Mummy was, and why she didn't come. Asked how she could have forgotten them, and why. Poor little kids, she thought now. And then there was Paul, and all the waiting she had done for him. And now here she was again. Waiting. Fucking waiting.

So now she would be cross-eyed driving, but so what? She'd survive if she was meant to. If not, so what. Again and again she drank deeply from the tall, thin glass, pushing the ice cubes back from her lips and teeth with her tongue and sucking the drops of liquid, liking the bite from the vodka and the tap of the glass against her teeth. Going inside and refilling it. She lit a cigarette off the end of the one she had been smoking, ground the butt out with her foot and tossed it into the begonias. She breathed in, filled her lungs with smoke from the new cigarette and held it in like a toke. Felt a wave of something descending. Grey cashmere. Exhaled, closed her eyes, lay back. And waited for her mother, who had been late all her life, not Viv. Barely alive in this ugly deadpan house with its dirty windows, its dusty ledges, its dead flies. Her mother as dried out and sharp as the dead brown pine needles, her mean spirit shrivelled up, rattling around in the bottom of her.

Whenever she was around her mother, she felt herself fill like a tidal bore with anger that gushed up from deep inside. Every time, she felt she might drown, so quickly she found herself thrashing around in it. Angry at the way she had learned to look at the world. With suspicion and mistrust so deep that with every breath she expected betrayal or disappointment. So defensive no one would ever get in without a crowbar or an axe. So fucking, fucking lonely, and a failure at being alone.

"No one's going to fuck with me again," she had promised as she turned the key in her apartment's lock for the first time. As she unloaded her car, as she lugged the bags of books for her university courses up the stairs. "Fucking never."

She had escaped, and she was a whole lot smarter now. She was twenty-four and she was together now, as hard as if she'd dipped herself in lacquer, and she didn't need goddam anyone. She was still working in a bar, true, but she was going to university, she was going to get a degree.

During the day she studied, read and wrote papers. She didn't have time for friends even if she'd made any. Up at the university she talked to her profs in class, but that was all. She needed to do well; she was on academic probation; she had to prove herself, or they wouldn't let her continue. At night she worked in a lounge as big as a tavern. Her face was hard, and she didn't smile, but her mind was quick and she knew how to give good service, so she made pretty good tips. She didn't like being outside, got home quickly with her smokes and books and bottles of wine. She didn't need anyone. Anyone. She kept her door locked. She copied out quotes and pinned them to her walls.

The Soul selects its own society, then Shuts the Door—

After work at two, three, four in the morning, her shirt sweaty and wrinkled, and booze and ashes on her black skirt and runs in her pantyhose, she knocked back a couple of black Russians or Caesars before she cabbed it home to crash and get up for nine o'clock Latin.

"Good insights," a professor wrote on her paper. "Interesting discussion," said another. "Good use of secondary sources." Slowly she began to accept their praise as genuine. Somewhere along the way in those four years she began to realize that her mother's judgment had always been the only one that mattered, and that she had always failed in her eyes. No more. Her mother's voice had always been the equivalent of the voice of God, her view the only one that counted, that ruled on her worth, her value. No more: now there were others. And how could her mother know anything about her, anyway? When had she ever known anything about her? And yet one letter from her could still negate everything in an instant, demolish her. She felt as though she were holding hell itself when she read her mother's letters, as though she held anger, not paper.

On her nights off work at the bar, she sat on her foamy with her books, a deck of smokes, her lighter, a big ashtray and a bottle of wine. She read—maybe Milton, or Vaughan—or watched her little black-and-white TV. And waited for that familiar feeling. That not caring, that going, going and gone.

When, in disgrace with fortune and men's eyes,
I all alone beweep my outcast state,
And trouble deaf heaven with my bootless cries,
And look upon myself and curse my fate.

The day before convocation, a letter from her mother had come, one of the bad ones. Lashing out at her for stuff she didn't even remember. The same old same old. She was about to get her degree, but it hadn't changed her mother. Not for a second. Fool that she was, she had thought it might be a letter of congratulations. It might even be a card. But no. It was a letter about universities. Her mother thought she might find it interesting to read the enclosed article. The article ranked the universities, and did she notice that the University of Calgary was nowhere near the top of the list? No one had ever pretended that the University of Calgary was Queen's, or McGill, or McMaster. But wasn't it interesting that it wasn't even UBC—or Edmonton!

She took the fifty dollars her father had sent as a graduation gift and went to the liquor store. The next morning, hungover, she had looked at herself in the mirror for a long time. It was stupid to go to convocation. It was stupid to get dressed up like some la la happy university graduate about to embark on life. What a fraud she was, what a failure no matter what she did. Nothing would ever be good enough. She saw beyond her greasy skin, her florid, puffy face, her bloodshot eyes and smudged mascara, her dirty, messy hair, her tight, hard line of a mouth. She saw herself as a chunk of granite: she was common, and hard. Black and white. Flung at someone, she'd gash a temple. She said aloud, evenly, staring into her eyes: "I hate you." And blinked. "You are a snivelling, pathetic thing," she said. And then she had found the resolve. Found her mother's inner fortitude and grim determination. "Get the razor," she said to her miserable image. "*Do you hear me?* Get it."

She glanced at the door her mother would come out. And then up at the stars, which were all swinging now, and she picked out the brightest. Then she looked down, to her body. She pulled up her shirt sleeves and took a long look at the tender slices and stitches on each of her wrists. Then she hid them again.

More than two decades had passed since she was a little girl so deeply in love with her mother no matter how she treated her; since her mother was the queen of her child's heart, so glamorous with her bright red lipstick, her velvet jackets, her sparkling brooches. Going off to the Queen Elizabeth Theatre, the symphony, the hospital ball. She and Amy standing in adoration as she got ready to go. Pressing their faces into the thick chocolate pile of her faux fur coat, asking for lipstick kisses that kept her close while she was gone. Oh, how she had loved her. In her gardening clothes, in those Black Watch plaid wool pants and that newly ironed yellow blouse, kneeling down to plant bulbs, daffodil and hyacinth; bending over to stake delphiniums, tie back the snowball bush. Talking to her African violets. Viv had loved her, and had loved watching her.

When her mother had carried her down the hall to her bath, had she loved her? When Viv crawled into her mother's bed to be safe from the witches that haunted her dreams, did she love her then? When her mother crouched down in front of her and straightened her white collar before she went to Sunday school, did she love her? Doing up the buttons on her green coat and folding down her white socks, did she love her? And as she screamed at her to *get out of her sight*, as she called her *useless* and *thoughtless* and *cruel*, as she shoved her, yelling *Go away!*, as she thrashed her, did she love her?

Every silence of her childhood deceptive and dangerous. Every day and every night. For as long as she could remember. Dreams of her mother with an axe. Dreams of her mother as a witch trying to grab her. What the hell was she doing here now?

Viv opened her eyes, gazed across the patio to the darkening shadows around the day lilies, then up, at the stars brightly swinging back and forth across the sky. That old and familiar little girl's longing inside. The wisps of longing for a mother who loved her, who was proud of her. But there was no other mother to have. This was the one. Between whose legs she had come into the world. And in that moment she wanted to dive into a deep pool of still water, she wanted to have grown in someone else's womb, to have been born a *beloved* daughter. This woman who had given her life made her wish she were dead every time she saw her.

"You don't have to stay. You could drive away," Viv said softly to herself, wiping away tears. "Just get in your car and drive away."

But then the back door opened and Pearl shuffled out. Hairspray, an acrid halo, floated over her head. She was carrying her gold purse and she was wearing her gold shoes. "I'm ready for the celebration," she said.

Partway to Chas's place, Viv stopped on the sidewalk to light a smoke, crossed to the boulevard in the centre of the street, sat down, and propped herself up against the trunk of one of the old trees and closed her eyes. She liked the feel of the trunk and the bark against her back, the feel of the ground beneath her. And when she opened her eyes again, she liked how the street lamps barely penetrated the branches of the heavily leafed old trees above her, which obscured the sky.

She loved Chas. She had met him down the street at the neighbourhood pub, and had gone home with him that night. He made her so happy; he was so nice; he was the nicest man she had ever met. When she woke up the next day, he was gone to his construction job and had left a note on the bedside table. *See you at lunch, honey-pie.* He brought her a burger, and a rose, and she got up to eat and drink coffee with him, and then she went back to his bed and slept again, her pounding head buried in the smell of one of his cast-off shirts.

If they stayed in the city on the weekend, they took a drive that became a ritual circuit. They started by driving past her grandparents' houses, then past Elbow Park elementary school where her mother and Aunt May had gone as children. Viv got out of the truck, walked over to the school's front door, imagined her mother going in those very doors all those decades ago. Six years old. Seven, eight, nine. Ten. Travelling through this very space, back and forth, back and forth.

On these drives she felt as though she was on some kind of a search, but had no idea about what or why. She wasn't curious about anything specific, but it was some kind of longing, and she was drawn to this repetition, this incantation, some attempt to stir something up she wanted, without knowing, to know. Other times they drove up north of Sixteenth Avenue to the graveyard where her grandparents were buried, and she and Chas might both get out of the truck and stand in front of the markers. What was one supposed to do? Sweep the dirt off, pull stray grass away. They did that. Then what? How were you supposed to honour your ancestors, grey ash beneath the grass, anyway? Who knew. Cheers, anyway, and she raised her Caesar.

"Is it Destiny that kept me here in Calgary, Chas, do you think? Am I *meant* to be here?" she asked him as they got back in the truck. "I mean, why didn't I move away? Why did I decide to stay in school?"

"Could be," Chas said, turning over the Dolly Parton cassette and then turning to her.

"Tighter," she said when he held her. "Tighter."

"No problem, Babe," he said.

He was the sweetest, most patient guy. Too nice, too patient sometimes. He didn't get anxious as they neared the bottom of a bottle, or the end of a deck of smokes. He could wait until tomorrow, and he was the same with everything—with sex, with food, with work. There was nothing he *had* to have, nothing he couldn't wait for. While she wanted everything right now. She wished he were just a bit stronger, wished he were a bit harder to please. He put up with her bullshit way too much and she found herself pushing to see just how far she could go. Too far. He needed to draw better lines. But no. After a few drinks he got all sweet and soft and mushy before he fell asleep, and when he woke up it was with an open, loving smile.

On other weekends they went for long drives out in the country in his old GMC truck, plugging cassettes of Randy Travis, the Forester Sisters, Dwight Yoakam into the tape deck and singing along. As they drove, they drank the Caesars they'd made up in batches on her kitchen counter and stashed in juice bottles they put in a car-sized cooler. They drove west to Bragg Creek, into the Kananaskis, to Banff, or south to Black Diamond, or Millarville. They drove, they got out and walked by the river, they came back to the truck for fresh drinks or a couple of tokes, and drove around some more. Going somewhere, going nowhere.

She was in grad school now, supposedly thinking complex literary thoughts, challenging her intellect, reading deeply, preparing presentations. Not killing more and more time with Chas. As they drove, she'd glance at her texts beside her on the seat, maybe tell him what she'd been reading about her specialty, the metaphysical poets, and she quoted some of them to set them in her mind, and told him why they were called that, and what the differences were among them. She taught him their names, and praised him like a pet when he could repeat them. Donne. Herbert. Marvell. Vaughan. Crashaw. And maybe, said some, Traherne. "Good boy!" she laughed. "Well done!"

"Woolf," said Chas. "Woof woof."

She told him what she was learning about love, and about the tug-of-war between bodily pleasure and the welfare of the soul in Henry Vaughan. She told him about Sir Philip Sidney, and the love between Astrophel and Stella. About Pound, and Stevens, and why they were so hard to access and why that was good, or bad, depending on what you thought about poetry. Was accessibility a crime or a virtue?

"You're getting good stuff into that pretty head of yours, aren't you?" Chas said proudly, with a loving smile. "But Vivvy—can you change a tire?"

On their first New Year's Eve, he showed up with red wine instead of white and she lost it. How many times had she said white? Didn't he know by now she hated red? She was so pissed off she called him a stupid fucking idiot and he left. And as he left, with the door wide open and other tenants in the foyer, he yelled at her for the first time.

"I don't fucking need this, Viv. I don't."

She slammed the door behind him. Her heart pounded with excitement. But he didn't come back. He didn't answer his phone, wouldn't come to his door or his window. His roommate, Teddy, half snapped and wearing a Santa hat, answered the front door with a smoke between his lips and a hot rum in his hand. "Sorry there, Vivvy. Not home. Well, home but not home. You know?"

At the corner store, she bought a deck of smokes with pennies and nickels she scrounged from all her pockets and then she sat on her couch, which, like all her furniture, had come from Chas, and looked around at the emptiness. No liquor. Nothing.

As midnight approached, she walked down to his house again. His truck was gone. The house was dark. The front door locked. His downstairs window was locked. What a bitch she was. She deserved to be locked out. She walked back to her apartment building down the alleys and heaved open the back door. Why was she like this? She went down the steps and closed her apartment door behind her and locked it. Stood alone in the silence. With a deep aching wish for her life not to be the way it was, for her not to be the way she was. What was the matter with her? She needed to somehow occupy the container that was her life differently. She needed to exorcise the nasty and mean someone crammed in here with her, crowding her out, breathing fire. Making her be a way her true self wasn't. She didn't know who she was sometimes, it was crazy, like she was possessed. If only Chas would. It would help. If only he wouldn't. Then, then she would be better, but first he had to. But what hope was there of that? That night she quit drinking.

On their honeymoon in Honolulu, she knew she should be happy, but she wasn't. At least not right now. Right now she was totally pissed off because her new husband had made no move to carry her over the threshold of the hotel room, no move to take her in his arms, to sweep her off her feet and make passionate I-can't-live-without-you, newly married, now-you-are-my-wife love to her the way she thought he should. He was waiting for her to get things going. Again. To make the decisions. Again. Why did he never take the initiative? Why was life always such a goddam struggle? Would she never be happy?

"What's with you, anyway?" she asked Chas. "Don't you *want* me?"

"Let's see, Viv," he said nicely, buttoning up his new Hawaiian shirt. "We just got married. We're in Hawaii on a honeymoon. What do *you* think?"

"What's the matter with you, then? Or better, what's the matter with *me*?"

He didn't answer. Just stood there, looking sad. And angry.

"What's the matter with me, Chas?" she prodded. "Why won't you touch me? Am I so repulsive?"

He shook his head.

"Jesus. You never fucking answer, Chas. You might as well be a deaf-mute for fuck's sake. Where's the joint?"

"In the ashtray," he said. "I'm going to the bar."

"Bar bar bar. Since I quit drinking, you always go to the bar. So fucking go, Chas. Avoid the issues. Just fucking go. Leave me here to have my honeymoon by myself."

And he did.

She slid the patio door open slowly and stepped out onto the cement balcony, where a white pigeon was perched on the railing. "Hey birdie," she said. The pigeon cocked its head and the sight was repulsive. There was no eye on the other side of its head, no feathers, just a gaping hole pecked into its skull, feathers, flesh, eye pecked off and out and down to the bone.

Chas turned on the TV right after his morning piss while he got ready for work and made his lunch. When he came back in the door from work, he had two numbers rolled and he handed her one and kissed her if she let him and held out the lighter. He cracked a beer and turned on the TV again to watch the game while she cooked them gourmet meals, which were followed by some crib and maybe a video. But if he was late and hadn't called to tell her, a blind fury rose in her and she pitched the food in the garbage as he came in the door. His friendly face turned livid, his grey face filled with thunder.

"You don't like me," he said, miserable, angry. "That's what it is, plain and simple, Viv. You don't like me."

"I like you, Chas. I *love* you with all my heart. More than anything on earth."

"You're pissed off all the goddam time about something. Do you know that? It's goddam impossible to make you happy."

"That isn't true. I'm not. If you would just—"

"Shut *up*, Viv! Give it a *rest. For fuck's sake.*"

"But really, Chas, it's the truth. Isn't it? There's always something you'd rather do than come home on time, isn't there?"

"No."

"Because who the fuck would want to come home to someone like me? Don't lie to me. Right? Right?" She followed him down the hall. "So. I'm not saying another word after this. After today. If you don't care, neither do I. You make me so goddam mad, Chas. I love you, but you piss me off so much I can't tell you."

"The whole world pisses you off, *Vivien*. And you piss your*self* off, too." And he slammed the door.

An hour later he came back, his eyes bloodshot. He was going to start the kitchen renos on the weekend, he said, and he would appreciate some input. A ceiling fan, a new kitchen counter, a bigger kitchen window. Would plain white paint do the trick? What did she want? Would she please just tell him what the hell she wanted?

She graduated and started teaching part-time. They bought a little house. They each had a vehicle. She liked buying him clothes; she liked buying music; she bought him a watch. On Friday nights he brought home flowers and Chinese and they got out the chopsticks and emptied every bowl and plate before they rolled over to the sofa to open their fortune cookies and watch TV until the double-fudge brownies were done and she loaded on the ice cream and chocolate sauce and brought them over. Goldie the engagement dog lazed between them on the couch, head on a knee, paw in a lap, and occasionally their hands touched as they petted him. Viv started running to keep the weight off, while Chas grew pudgy. She grew to love running, loved how invigorating it was, the growing distance she could cover. She became as proportionately lean as she had been when she was a child, when she could feel her bones beneath her flesh and muscle. If she ran angry, she ran better, faster. Now, if she could find a way to do that with the rest of her life.

"This is the good life," Chas said. "We're living it, honey."

Nice to see that you have finally settled down, wrote her mother. I attribute that fully to Charles. Charles is a fine fellow. Steady. Reliable. Charles is just what you need.

"I am bored out of my fucking skull," she said to the mirror.

"You just can't live without some bloody drama going on," Chas said behind her. "You should have been an actress. You're wired with drama. I don't think you even *want* to be happy, do you?"

"Actor. Of course I don't want to be happy, Chas. Why would I? What do you think? To be blunt, what I want is to get laid. You haven't kissed me in weeks."

"You think I'm crazy? You think I'm going to climb into a chipper? When's the last time you kissed me?"

"Right. This is going nowhere fast, *Charles.* You know, the more you pull away, the worse it's going to get. I'm serious."

The day the semester ended, Viv, furious at Chas over his obvious rejection of her, rolled some joints, hopped in the van and headed for the coast. In under an hour she had fled her mother's. The bitch. Why had she gone there, anyway? Viv was barely in the door when her mother handed her a list. Not even a hello, Vivien, how nice to see you. No how was your trip. No would you like a cup of tea. It was clean the eavestroughs. Take out the garbage. Sweep the sidewalks. "You had better concentrate on getting changed into your work clothes," her mother had said in greeting. "You're late." Put it on a fucking placard, Mother.

What the hell had she thought would happen? That her mother would be understanding? Give her marital advice? Console her? Fat chance. But Viv had tried, anyway. "I am having some trouble in my marriage, Mum," she had said from the stepladder. "I don't know what to do." And what happened then? Her mother told her that whatever it was, it was her own fault. That Viv should look to herself, to her own behaviour, for an answer to that. Viv could have dropped crap from the eavestroughs onto her head but she resisted. She should have known her mother would take his side. Was she out of her fucking skull for going there with some weird form of tattered and bleeding hope? Practically begging for help? What a suck she was.

Approaching the exit for Beresford, she lit a joint and rolled down the window. Trees along the roadsides tossed in a building wind. The clouds were dark and low. Viv drove the six miles down 200th Street and stopped the van on the side of the road near their old place and got out. The big chain-link gate was locked, but she refused to be deterred and her anger propelled her over the high barbed wire fence and she jumped down, started walking down the gravel pit road that would lead to the property line.

The oldest nightmare she could remember had taken place on this road. In the dream, instead of turning up their driveway, Pearl had come in here, which was puzzling because she never came in here. It was pitch-dark, and Pearl had stopped the car on the deserted gravel road. She put on the emergency brake, turned off the lights and turned towards Viv. Pearl's eyes gleamed in the dark with a wild and white craziness, and Viv's heart stopped. Her mother was going to kill her.

Now, instead, she wished someone would kill her mother, bash her fucking head in. Viv strode more quickly, anger still pulsing. Why did no one ever take her side? Why was she still so fucking stupid about her mother? Why couldn't she ever, ever get it through her thick head and give up?

She felt better the moment she breathed the air in what had been their part of the woods, as though her body recognized the place in her lungs; as though the woods remembered her and still belonged to her, and her to them. Her body remembered how to move through the woods, how to push branches out of the way while bending, while turning; when to step on, step over, push through. Here, she couldn't get lost no matter how deep she went into thickets and forest.

And then she was home. Home, at the heart of the property. Home, in the tree roots where she had curled up and found comfort. When she was six eight ten twelve thirteen fourteen and then. She stopped, closed her eyes and listened as the rain started to come heavily, slapping against the vine maple leaves, dripping from evergreen branches then soaking her hair and her coat. "Don't cry," she whispered, sitting down in the cubbyhole formed by the roots and wrapping her arms around herself. Please don't cry.

She felt calm when she again raised her head, when she saw her child-self up ahead running towards her from the log that crossed over the creek, running towards this forest all those days all those years all those times ago, along those familiar paths, now gone, grown over. She knew the trees, knew the tall old green beside the dead gold grasses of last year's meadow. She knew this place better than she knew anywhere else on earth, and it knew her. Here she was again, all these years later, again seeking solace. She stood and moved on towards the creek, where she expected to be able to glimpse the house from its banks. But the trees had grown huge, and her view was blocked by trunks, branches, leaves and ferns.

The rain became a downpour as she drove to her father's. From one house to the other, she thought, from her mother's to her father's, like she was a clothesline screwed in tight at both ends and heavy laden with dripping wet clothes. Her mother's rotting deck and pine needles, her constant complaining and criticism. Her father's stinky old planter boxes, his negativity and his rye. And Scotch. And gin. The fucking north and south poles of her life. What the hell was going on? Where did she belong?

"Have you been crying, dear?" her father asked solicitously, greeting her at the front door.

"Yes," she snuffled.

"Has someone been unkind to you?"

"My mother. Of course. Do you have any Kleenex, Dad?"

"I have this—will this do?" He took a clean pressed handkerchief from inside his suit jacket. "Has she, dear?"

"Thanks. Don't sound so surprised. Of course she has. When is she *ever* anything else?" She sobbed against his chest. "Oh, Daddy. She has *always* been mean to me. *Always.*"

"Dear heart. I'm sorry to hear that." He patted her shoulder. "Come in. What have you been doing to get so wet? Maybe you should get changed. I think that what you need is a drink. Would you like a drink? I'm having one."

She pulled angrily away. "I don't drink. Remember? Why don't you ever remember, Dad?" She followed him into the house and up the stairs. "Dad? Why didn't you help us? When we were little, why didn't you tell her to stop being so wretchedly bloody awful to us? Dad?"

"I didn't know, dear! I was at work, you know."

"Not all the time, you weren't. Not at night, and on weekends."

He paused, spoke more coolly. "Well, I don't know about that. Maybe I was on call. Would you like a drink or not?"

"*No!* I told you. You never listen to me."

"I do, dear."

"Dad, Mum was horrible to you too. You *must* remember that. And surely you must have been able to figure out that if she treated you like that, chances were you weren't the only one. Or did you just *believe* her when she said we were just plain *bad*?"

"Dear, you are sounding quite fierce and you've only just arrived. I don't remember her saying that." He opened the fridge.

"How convenient for you."

"What was that?"

"Nothing."

In the bedroom that used to be hers, she found a hot pink track suit of Amy's in the closet. Amy, Amy. She announced her presence everywhere, oh sweet and obedient daughter, and unlike Viv, was welcomed and at home everywhere she went. Must be nice to have the "good" market cornered. Must be nice to be so nice. Viv peeled off her wet clothes and put on the track suit. It was too big and she hated pink.

"You look better, dear," her father said when she entered the living room. "Less dishevelled, overall. Certainly dryer. Pink is a nice colour on you. Now sit down over here. I have something to show you. Have you heard about Cecilia Bartoli? She's quite a girl. With quite the voice. Everyone's talking about her, you know." He waved the video box in Viv's face.

"Don't, Dad. I've seen that video about ten times."

"She's a lovely girl. I don't think you've seen this one. Not this particular one. Sit back down, dear, and I'll put it on for you. It'll take your mind off things."

"I said I've seen it."

"I'm sure you haven't."

"Dad, I just got here. I don't want to watch TV."

"Sit down on the couch and watch this video with me. You'll feel better."

"No, thank you."

He stood up. "Vivien—"

"Dad! Quit telling me what to do all the time!"

"You are really quite fierce," he said mildly, as the video began and Bartoli's voice filled the room. "You know, Vivien, you can't possibly fight the whole world. And I think you are fighting it more than it is fighting you. Make love not war, you know that bumper sticker, dear? Now be a good guest and sit down."

The idea of their mother's falling in love at all—or anyone's falling in love with her—verged on the obscene. Viv had laughed when Amy called to tell her. "Who with? With whom? You have *got* to be kidding," she said. But there was Pearl, and there was Roger Werner. (Where had she found him? Surely not at the hairdresser's, she and Amy giggled. Did she meet him at Safeway? At the doctor's?) And now, after a mere six months' courtship, they were getting married. Pearl's giddy behaviour, which included a rusty kind of giggling on the phone, was unsettling. Her attempts at being coy with wedding details, her bizarrely girlish response to Roger's mooning and fawning over her (which was so odd in itself), were downright strange. But. Maybe a transformation was possible. None of her daughters would have believed it to be possible, but it was beginning to seem that they were wrong. Miracles did happen, right? She certainly seemed happier, said Amy. Well, maybe now they could visit without going into emotional contortions, said Ruby, while Laurel's comment was that maybe now they would be able to have a real relationship with their mother. Dream on, said Viv. But. Maybe she was mistaken. And it seemed to be so: during the coming year Pearl seemed capable of being genuinely nice.

On her first visit to her mother in her new married state, Vivien hadn't felt the weight of dread descend as she turned in her mother's driveway, and what an amazing, hopeful feeling that absence was. And then the sun had come out and spattered the driveway with light. Pearl hadn't answered the door, and since for once it was unlocked, Viv just went right in, thinking that maybe the light and the unlocked door would prove to be symbolic of her mother's rebirth, her enormous and astounding change of heart and mind. A change of essential character. Who could have predicted such power in love? She could hear her mother talking to someone down in her bedroom, and wondered if Roger hadn't gone to visit his son after all. She was at first unable to distinguish words—she heard only her mother's familiar, monotonous voice boring the walls and floating lethargically down the hall like a lazy carp. Viv put her bag down in the living room, took a deep breath and tiptoed down to peer into her mother's bedroom. Her mother was sitting alone on the edge of her bed with one of her jewellery boxes open beside her, the blue leather one with the suede pillows inside. She was just lifting out a pair of gold earrings and a chain, which, she was telling an invisible audience, she would wear when she went out for dinner with her youngest daughter, Vivien, who was late.

"Hi, Mum," Vivien said, entering.

"Oh. It's you." Her mother's voice was completely flat.

"May I come in?"

"I don't see why not."

Vivien approached the bed. "What are you doing, Mum?"

"What does it look like I'm doing? I'm getting ready for dinner. My aunt Pearly K, after whom I am named, used to show me her jewellery when I was a little girl."

Viv sat down beside her mother, made the bed bounce a little, and Pearl frowned.

"I remember," Viv said, "how you let Amy and me see in your jewellery boxes when we were small. You'd open them on your bed just like this. We loved it, too. It was like the treasure in Aladdin's cave, I used to think. So magical. Special."

Pearl looked again at the pieces of gold jewellery she was holding in her crooked, gnarled hands. "Your sister Amethyst owes me a letter," she said. "You all do." Then she said, "The K stood for Klondike, after the gold rush that started the year she was born. She hated her name."

"I would have too. Klondike. Imagine!"

"I thought it was a rather clever idea."

"I guess. Mum? I also remember how you'd get dressed up to go out, to go into the city, and I'd think you were the most beautiful mother in the whole world. I was so proud of you." Vivien paused. Her mother said nothing. Feeling a mild desperation, Viv went on. "You know, I can feel your velvet jacket against my cheek if I think about it. I can feel the thick, furry pile of that chocolate brown fake fur coat you used to wear. I can smell your VO5 hairspray, and your Max Factor powder, and I can see the bright poppy red of your lipstick. Mum?"

Pearl was looking into space. "Your father liked those hospital balls. Beresford high society. Ha! I detested them. They were a trial."

"Amy and I always liked it when you left us a kiss on our cheeks with your lipstick. Remember? And remember how you wore a French roll for a while? I thought that was so elegant." Viv stopped then, and for a while there was nothing at all in the stale, disturbed air. Then Pearl, who had still not acknowledged her daughter's opening of her heart, rose, and slowly made her way over to her dressing table, took two more boxes out of the second drawer and brought them over to the bed. One red box, one grey.

"My aunt Pearly K never married. She should have; *she* would have made a wonderful mother. But when she was a young woman, she acquired an appointment working for an MP in Ottawa, and off she went to see the capital. However. Shortly after she started the job, the man made inappropriate advances towards her, and she packed up and came right home. She stayed in Winnipeg after that, and became a dental assistant, which proved much more satisfactory."

"And that was it for men?" Viv asked, admiring three of her mother's dinner rings on her hands.

"You can put those back. She did become engaged once, but she broke it off. His name was Wherrit, and he worked in a bank."

"Maybe that's why in the pictures she looks so sad."

"*I* wouldn't hazard a guess as to the reason. *I* wouldn't have said she looked sad. And I wouldn't say she was unhappy, either. She liked the horse races. And wearing stripes."

"I like looking at your old photo albums," said Viv. "May I see one?"

"I don't," said Pearl.

Viv flopped back on the bed and stared at the light fixture on the ceiling. Her mother could suck the joy out of Jesus. Why couldn't she be nicer? The light fixture was full of bugs, and one of the light bulbs was out. Still, she was a million percent better than she had been before Roger came along. Viv could see cobwebs in the corners of the ceiling. She could see a big fat spider. Waiting.

"I barely know what's in here anymore," Pearl said, returning to her project. Slowly she unzipped grubby satin bags, opened the soiled drawstrings of flannelette pouches, unwrapped wrinkled old tissue paper and lifted out more strings of beads, brooches, earrings and chains.

"That French roll hairdo was a ridiculous amount of work."

Viv rolled over on her side and reached over to pick up a yellow sparkly brooch with matching earrings and lined the three pieces up on the bedspread. She put on another ring, one with a large pale green stone. "These were my favourites when I was small," she said.

Pearl picked up a bracelet made of rectangular stainless steel blocks and draped it over her wrist. "Your father gave me this. On a day when he was feeling artsy." Then she looked up and said bitterly, "When I was having a miscarriage in my parents' house, your precious father was downstairs in the living room *playing the damned piano*. The nurse attending me was afraid to interrupt him to ask if she could give me heroin for the pain. In the end she gave it to me anyway, *without* his permission. Ha! Imagine ignoring the plight of his wife! And him a doctor. Right in my parents' house in Calgary, on Montcalm Crescent." Pearl gave her daughter a look as though she blamed her and stuffed the bracelet into a pink satin bag and zipped it up.

"Mum?"

"What is it?"

"When Dad proposed, why didn't you say no?"

Pearl answered slowly, guardedly, "Well, no one else had asked me."

"So? You weren't exactly over the hill."

"You have to marry *someone*."

"No you don't."

Pearl looked at her daughter hard. "Well, a lesbian wouldn't marry, I suppose."

Viv laughed. "But did you even *like* each other? Ever? Did you have anything at all in common?"

"We played badminton. Our fathers both worked for the CPR."

"And that's it?"

"Well," Pearl said, a strange coy smile in her voice. "There was a strong . . . sexual attraction." She looked Viv in the eye. "*You* would understand *that*."

"Yes," Viv said, mortified.

"*And* do you know what else?" Pearl said, still looking at Viv as if assessing the wisdom of confiding in her. "Your father's mother told me that I must 'make myself available' to my husband in bed *every night*—and you know what *that* means."

Viv laughed. Again. Had she ever laughed in this house before? "Good thing you were sexually attracted, then."

Pearl paused, gave Viv an icy look and said, "I don't know why you find this all so amusing."

"I don't—it's just that you've never told me most of this before and I'm excited. Maybe even happy. And a little nervous."

"I see. Well, here is something else. Eleanor Mayfield, your grandmother, loved to give advice, and she gave me much more than I needed or wanted. And she was a very good bridge player. When your father and I were engaged, she kept trying to get me to take up bridge. But I did not, and do not, like playing bridge. Nor did I join the ladies' auxiliary or the church choir in Banff, much to her chagrin."

"Mum? Did you ever have an engagement ring? I don't remember your having one."

"Yes, I did. I didn't like it, though. The one from Roger is much nicer."

"What happened to the one from Dad? Have I ever seen it?"

"No, you haven't. It was more from his mother than from him, if you must know. What happened to it? Bill Garbageman came right into the house one day and took it from beside the kitchen sink."

"Bill Garbageman?! Why would Bill Garbageman have come into the house?"

"Don't ask me."

"But how would he even know your ring was there?"

"How would *I* know? *I* wouldn't presume to know how a garbageman's mind works."

Pearl began bundling the jewellery back up, replacing it somewhat roughly in the bags and boxes, as though every piece, compounded by the presence of this daughter, caused her a struggle.

When she closed the doors of her dressing table, she turned to Viv and said, "Now you can tell me about my fine son-in-law. How is Chas? Why didn't he come with you?"

By the second year of their marriage, Pearl had reverted to her old self and was treating Roger, and her daughters, like absolute shit. The mooning and fawning had all been crap. Of course. They had all been duped, and poor Roger was stuck with her. "Yes, dear," he said, chipper in his humility, in his inability to do anything right. "I'm sorry, dear." What a crock it all had been. She was a bitch, she had always been a bitch, she had just tricked them for a while.

And then the bad news came: Roger had lung cancer. He was going to die. He couldn't stop coughing; he spat into a basin; the sounds of his retching drove Pearl wild. But in the end it wasn't the cancer that killed him. One day, after disembarking the HandyDART bus and dismissing the driver, Pearl and Roger had made their way arm in arm across the cement patio to the steps. The three steps, up to their back door, that Roger had wanted to put railings on but Pearl had refused. "*No*," she had said. "How many times do I have to tell you? I am *not* going to fall. Stop pestering me." That afternoon they fell off the steps and landed on the concrete.

"He has so little to say now," Pearl complained once her cracked pelvis had healed and she was released from the hospital. "It is impossible to have a decent conversation. I sit there. He lies there. He doesn't say a word anymore, and so I can't tell if he can even hear me. And every time it's twenty dollars by taxi!"

"But how is he?" Viv asked. "How is his fractured skull? How is the cancer?"

"How is he? Don't ask me. No one bothers to call and let me know. Why don't you ask me how *I* am doing? I could answer that, if anyone cared."

"Maybe they think *you* don't care."

"Did you tell them that?"

"No. Have you called the hospital?"

"Why should I?"

After Roger's funeral, Viv drove Pearl back to her house, and before the others arrived she said, "Maybe now you'll get a goddam railing, Mum. It could happen again, you know."

"That's a heartless thing to say. But coming from you I shouldn't be surprised. *No.* I've faced enough change for now."

"Mum, I think—"

"No one cares what you think. I least of all."

"Mum—"

"Shut your trap and mind your own business. Help me into the house."

"*Don't* get a goddam railing, Mum."

"What did you say?"

"Nothing."

Evelyn stood in the foyer of The Manor welcoming her guests, her tall black beehive glistening, her long black skirt beautifully pressed, a replica cameo pinned high in the centre of the collar of her lace-trimmed white blouse. "Good evening, Pearl," she said. "So nice to see you."

"Good evening," said Pearl. Evelyn smiled benevolently and took Pearl's coat, and then Viv's. Evelyn's husband, Marcel, emerged from the kitchen wearing his chef's hat. He kissed Pearl's hand. Pearl beamed. *They* certainly knew how to please her. Pearl and Viv followed Evelyn's gliding figure past the other customers to what had been Pearl and Roger's favourite booth, the last one, at the back of the restaurant, near the big mirrors.

"My daughter may need a menu, but I don't," said Pearl. "I am very hungry. I will have the creamed seafood *en cassoulet*."

"A very good choice," said Evelyn.

"I so like the scallops," Pearl beamed again.

Once Evelyn was gone, she turned to Vivien and the light went out of her face as she said sharply, "I have something to say to you and you are not to interrupt."

"All right."

"It concerns my husband's will."

Viv's heart lurched. She felt capable of murder when she thought about Roger's will. She had promised Chas, promised herself that she would keep her mouth shut no matter what. Poor old Roger. Now, in addition to his shortened life, his will had been declared invalid because of some technical detail and so Pearl could legally keep *everything*, no matter what Roger had said he wanted for his sons. The sons had asked if they might have some of Roger's clothes—a hand-tooled leather belt he had liked; a tie one of them had given him on his seventy-fifth birthday. They asked if they could have his special egg cup, and a photo album from when they were children. A plaster dog that had sat on their fireplace hearth. "No, you may not," Pearl said. "Not a thing." She threw out the photo album. She sent the clothes to the church thrift sale by taxi. The jewellery, some of it valuable and all of it intended for Roger's sons' wives, was in her jewellery boxes. She talked to the Mexican plaster dog and stroked it on the head and put a dish of water down beside it. "Don't tell me I don't have a sense of humour," she said.

Now at dinner she said, "*I* believe I have acted, and am acting, fairly," and she took a confident sip of her cocktail, a Planter's Punch. "First of all, I am aware that you think I have acted badly about the jewellery. But you do not know Roger's sons or their wives. I have never seen either Charlena or Janice in anything other than blue jeans. Ever. They *cannot* appreciate jewellery."

"That doesn't matter," Viv said angrily, breaking her vow and hating herself. "You know what he wanted. He wrote it all down."

"The lawyers have told me I don't *have* to do anything, and no one can make me. Least of all you."

"You wouldn't even give them his *egg cup*, for Christ's sake. Or his *belt*."

Pearl took a confident sip and said, "Well, listen to you on your high horse. You're a fine one to be telling me what is right and wrong. Who do you think you are?"

"Nobody. Is that the right answer?"

"It is. I am not about to listen to the likes of you. You may as well be quiet. Think what you like."

"I *will* think what I like," Viv hissed, choking now with fury. "I think you are *wicked*. I *hate* it that you are my mother."

Viv slid out of the booth and headed for the washroom. She sat on the toilet with her head in her hands. "Just leave," she whispered. "Just fucking leave. Get out of here. Go."

But she didn't. She was trying to be different. She was trying not to get involved, not to get embroiled, ensnared. She was trying to stand back and observe, she was trying to rise above, or transcend. She washed her face and dried it on the rough brown paper towels and returned to the booth, taking long, deep breaths. Her mother said in a meek, little-old-lady voice, "You were gone a long time."

Vivien's jaw moved, but she didn't speak. She crunched the ice cubes from her empty glass like bones.

"It is my turn now," Pearl said, laying down her fork and placing her neatly folded serviette beside it. Her plate was almost full. Vivien's was empty. She couldn't have said what she had ordered or eaten. Vacuumed, was more like it. She wasn't doing so well on her pledges to be unaffected, was she? So much for progress. Pearl slid out of the booth, stepped carefully down onto the carpet and slowly made her way along the aisle towards the washroom. Vivien closed her eyes. How stressed are you? she asked herself. The only time the desire to drink got this bad was when she was around her mother. She ordered another Perrier. She kept her eyes closed and took more deep breaths.

"Vivien! Vivien!" There was urgency in her mother's voice. Viv opened her eyes and looked over. Pearl was standing in the middle of the restaurant in her white slip. Her red and gold skirt was around her ankles, and she was trapped: she couldn't move forward or backward because the skirt was in the way, and she wasn't flexible enough to reach down to pull it up. Her eyes met her daughter's. She looked down at herself. Their eyes met again.

Then Vivien started to laugh. She laughed so hard she couldn't breathe. She attempted to leave the booth, but she broke up again, laughed, and laughed, and laughed until finally, finally she could move. "*Mum!*" she whispered as she came up to her, gasping for air, guts aching. "Your skirt fell off!"

Pearl snickered then too. "*I know that!* Do you think I don't *know* that?! Help me!"

They were both laughing then, both bent over, fooling with the silky red and gold outfit. Vivien managed to pull the skirt up and get it rebuttoned, but she was gasping and dizzy from embarrassment and lack of oxygen. Pearl, however, had regained her composure, and she shook her daughter off and raised her head high, pointedly ignored everyone in the restaurant as she continued her trip to the ladies' room. Still giggling, Vivien returned to the booth, her guts tight and clenched, her face red. She picked up her water glass and held it against her cheek. The coldness felt good. She couldn't stop laughing. Then the bathroom door opened and Pearl emerged.

Vivien watched her mother's slow progress as she began her return trip, and she felt gales both of laughter and of tears welling up in her again. She stifled them both, and in that moment she had to admit that in spite of it all, she sometimes admired her mother. She had to admire how Pearl could totally ignore what people thought and keep going. Keep doing what to her was *right.* Even when it meant taking on the world.

Goldie, over eight, greying in the muzzle, stiff in the hips and cloudy in the eyes, stood beside her on the bluff. Viv closed her eyes and felt the brisk wind blowing. She was facing east, towards Saskatchewan. The dog was close against her leg. It would be so hard to leave him behind. Chas too, though he'd never believe it if she told him. He'd never believe that she still loved him, either. He'd say she had a funny way of showing it.

Coming in from the garage, Chas had stepped around the stacks of boxes on his way to the fridge. He had cracked a beer, and paused to pat Goldie, lying beside her, and then he had headed back out. The door didn't close properly behind him and it swung open, and she could hear Randy Travis on the portable stereo. "Diggin' Up Bones." Goldie got up from beside her, stretched, glanced at her, and followed Chas out.

For their last supper she cooked the turkey from the freezer downstairs. She bought cheese buns from the Glamorgan bakery. She steamed green beans, made a Caesar salad with lots of garlic. Got out the one specially labelled bottle of wine left over from their wedding: he might as well drink it. She lit long purple tapers left over from Easter, she put on the Steve Miller Band and called Chas to the table, set with their white wedding china, cloth serviettes and two of their four crystal glasses, water for her, wine for Chas.

The salad was good. The cheese buns were good. But she had overcooked the beans while she was making the gravy, which was lumpy and had to be strained. The turkey had been in the freezer too long and the flavour was odd and the meat such a strange texture neither of them wanted to eat it. Chas opened the wine, tasted it, grimaced. "Skunky," he said, and their eyes met. Before he dumped it down the toilet, he proposed a toast. "To the future," he said.

You're making a mistake, her mother typed onto plain white paper. *You were lucky to get him and mark my words you'll regret this.*

Viv looked out the back door at their garden, at the tomato plants, the bank of sweet peas, the bird bath. At the rows of lettuce and carrots, at the hills of potatoes. So much in a small space. She looked up at the inchworms dangling from the tree, at the spiderweb beside the gate. At Frank's gardening shoes side by side, and at her clogs, askew. Frank. With him she had finally recognized herself; with him she had finally become who she truly was. She had shivered with joy. Her guts had been snakes. Because of him, because of her move eastward, she had been born, finally; she was fully, completely alive. Farther from home than she had ever been, she had found home. She had never realized she had the *capacity* to feel like this.

They were the same height, the same build, the same colouring; their hands and feet were the same size. When they lay together, when they twined and arched, they fit. On long walks by the South Saskatchewan River he talked, they talked, she talked, their thoughts and voices tumbling together. Art. Music. Ideas. Books. Each other. They sat on the couch listening to the CBC. Home. She was home. This was her chance, she knew; her chance, quite probably her last, to get it right, her last chance to make someone happy instead of miserable. Herself included. Finally, finally she had found the right man, and she became the right woman.

But. How wrong, how terribly wrong, she had been. And how quickly it was revealed. Less than a year. Less than six months before the truth surfaced and did not submerge again. All her faults and flaws had not taken flight. Trouble had not fallen away. No. No. Beneath her delusions of rebirth she was forced to see that she was the same as she had been. As she had always been.

"I don't know how much more of this I can take," Frank had said again, loudly and firmly.

"Neither do I," she had retorted hotly. "The problem is perfectly obvious to me, if not you: you just don't love me."

"How can you believe that? If I didn't love you, why would I put up with all this? Why would I even be *talking* about having a baby with you?"

"I'm sorry. Frank, I'm really sorry."

"You know what, Viv? You wouldn't know love if it came in wearing a sign."

And he left the room. Now he wouldn't speak to her for days. He would pass her silently. Wouldn't touch her. Was cold as a ghost if she touched him. As though he didn't feel her at all. As though for him, and therefore the world, she didn't exist. That's how he fought. And she would lie next to him at night sobbing, and he would do nothing. His heart would not soften. "I have to get some sleep," he said.

This time had been one of the worst, and he probably hated her now and it served her right. He had thrown a cantaloupe; little seeds and fragments of its flesh were stuck to the kitchen wall. She felt sick with self-loathing. What a bitch she was, how wrong she was, when two hours ago she would have wagered her life she was right. How was she supposed to tell? How could she trust herself? Ever? Surely sometimes she was right, wasn't she? Ever? She couldn't tell. Couldn't stand back from herself and see. Why was she like this? She had to live alone, she had sobbed, she had to keep away, she would be better dead than harming if she couldn't stop herself.

She lay down on the living room floor, on the worn maple hardwood beside the empty fireplace. She saw again the hurt and frustration in Frank's face. She saw again Chas's kind face, full of pain and sadness, shaking her hand goodbye. Saw Barry as she kissed him on the cheek and got out of his car for the last time. Cruelty and love, cruelty and love. What was at the heart of it? How sorry she was, how completely sorry for how badly she had treated them yet at the same time she had loved them, each with all her heart. Nothing had been their fault. No. It was her, her and her anger, her very own goddam anger, sliding into and out of her like ugly, strong eels. Wrapped around her ankles, twined round her body. The truth was that she was unchanged. The same cruel words flew from her lips and found their mark.

How wrong she had been. Angry, hateful, hurtful, her goddam mother was there, living, curled up inside her like a snake. Oh God. Was she doomed? Would she *never* be shed of her?

Viv rolled over on her side, felt the hardwood floor unyielding against her hip. How utterly, utterly ridiculous she was. She had spent her life defending herself, protecting herself, fighting against her mother with everything she had, determined not to become like her. What a fool. She had not inherited black hair or blue eyes the way Ruby and Amy had; she had not inherited a lilting, musical voice like Laurel's. Instead, she had this anger. There was no denying it, no avoiding it, no turning a blinded eye or blaming anyone else. She, she was the source.

April a year later. The garden was still dead, the icy paving stones cold under her bare feet as she ran out to the compost and back. Broken stalks poking through the remaining snow. Spring seemed a long way off. Still plenty of cold and dark to get through first.

Over the winter, a glacier-like moving forward. Not meaning cold, or even slow—but solid, wide, affecting the entire wide terrain of her. A growing awareness that what Frank said was often not what she heard, that she twisted it, warped it, saw only the negative potential in the meaning. That people were generally kind, their intentions good, not suspect.

She had never been more determined to change. She had to change: her life depended on it. And her baby's life. She *had* to change so that she would never do to the child now growing inside her what had been done to her, and the strength of this desire forced her irrevocably forward, grinding earth and sharp stones of regret deep into her.

That September, as labour began, and she and Frank looked out the huge hospital windows at the perfect autumn day, at the blue sky and blue river, the golds and browns along the banks, the physical memory of that first birth resurfaced in her body and sucked her back in time. This birth. That birth. The red and black pain. Back again. Identical. The fear, too. That baby, this baby. That young woman, the girl she had been; the much different woman she was now. If she could just have five minutes, she remembered thinking. If this possession, this blinding, overwhelming pain could just stop for five minutes so that she could get a grip. But it was like trying to stop swimming in a swift-moving river, and the to her chaotic rhythms of birthing did not stop until she saw the baby emerging from her body, saw the black hair, saw the umbilical cord joining them together.

The doctor wrapped the baby and placed her on her chest. Viv held the baby close, close. She hummed to her as she learned to nurse, kissed her sweet face, her head, her hands, any part of her she could. And felt this joy, this overwhelming joy over the gift of this particular life. She—she!—was a mother. This baby, this girl, her Messiah. A mother, and this baby, Stella, would get the best she could give her.

"You have to take her to see her grandparents," Frank said. "You can't wait until she's in university."

"I don't want her to see Mum. I don't want Mum to touch her, contaminate her. I don't want her anywhere near her, I want to keep her safe."

"She'll have to see her eventually."

"I don't want her to."

Through the lighted window, Viv could see her mother sitting in profile at her kitchen table. She reminded her of Miss Emily Grierson in the Faulkner story, though her mother was certainly no icon. Pearl was staring into space, and she was wearing her camel hair coat, and was clearly ready to go out. Viv stood in the shadow of the house and watched through the window for a few moments. Pearl didn't move, and Viv wondered how long she had been sitting there. She wasn't reading; she was just staring at the surface of the table, at the cover of a closed book. She was ossified, perhaps. Or dead. But when Viv knocked on the window, Pearl readily rose to unlock the back door. Viv forced a smile and commented that her hair looked very nice. Pearl said it had been done the day before. Viv then asked her where she was getting her hair done these days. "You don't need to know everything," Pearl said. "Especially when you are so late. Where's the baby? Where is Stella Louise?"

"I left her at home. Frank is looking after her."

"I expressly wanted you to bring her!"

"I'm sorry. She couldn't come. She has a cold. Next time. Next time, I'll bring her."

"What do men know about babies? I won't be able to give her her Christmas present."

"I'll take her the present for you. And I'll send you a picture. I'm sorry."

Viv poured them each a Coke, spiked her mother's with rum and carried them into the living room, which seemed particularly dark and empty in spite of the poinsettia Ruby had left on the coffee table. Viv asked where the TV and the console stereo had gone. Pearl, still wearing her coat, took the drink and said that she didn't require those pieces of furniture anymore, and had sold them. She sat down and gestured that Viv should do the same. "Reading is now my primary extracurricular activity," Pearl said, sipping her drink, "though perhaps the right phrase is simply 'curricular.'" Then she asked Viv to put up her outdoor Christmas lights, adding, "I had thought I could mind the baby while you did it, but that clearly isn't about to happen now." Viv said that she couldn't put up the lights in the dark in heels and a dress. Pearl wasn't pleased with this news, and said, "Surely someone with character could overcome such obstacles if he really wanted to. Where there's a will, there's a way, et cetera. But apparently not in this case."

"Apparently not," Viv agreed. Pearl heaved a great sigh of defeat. Might Viv be able to bring herself to help put up the Christmas tree, then, or was *that* beyond her too?

"I can do that," Viv said. "But now? I thought we were going out for supper."

"*No, not now!*" Pearl said with exasperation, putting her drink down on a coaster with a thud. "*After* dinner, of course! I am *very* hungry because you are so late, and I *want* to go *now*! Ye gods!"

"Don't you want to finish your drink, Mum? It has rum in it."

"I know it has rum in it. I'm not a moron. I don't *want* it right now. Right now I am *hungry*. As I've just finished saying! Are you deaf? And I am getting hot in this coat." She stood up.

When Pearl removed her coat at The Manor and handed it to Evelyn, Viv saw that her mother was wearing four brooches and that they were pinned every which way onto her dress. She was wearing two very different bracelets—the one made of stainless steel rectangles that Viv's father had given her years ago and the stretchy one with the sparkly baubles—on the same wrist. And she was wearing what must have been all of her necklaces—gold, silver, shells, stones, medallions—more than a dozen of them. All those together must be heavy around an old person's neck, Viv thought. And then she thought about what hard work it must have been getting all that on, with the arthritis in her mother's hands so bad. She wondered vaguely if something was the matter.

"You're looking festive," Viv said.

"What is that supposed to mean?" Pearl said, and, turning to the waiter Evelyn had sent over, ordered a Singapore sling. "How is Stella?" she asked next. "How is my erstwhile son-in-law?"

"He's more than erstwhile, Mum. And Stella is just fine. Getting very chatty. Was I chatty when I was a baby, Mum?"

"Probably. I remember that you wanted to be held every second and what a trial that was, what with Amethyst's allergies and asthma needing attending to. Where is Amethyst? I thought she'd be here by now."

There was definitely something the matter. When Viv asked if she was ready for another drink or whether she'd prefer some wine, she responded by quoting a line or two from a poem by Archibald Lampman, "Godspeed to the Snow," which he had written in April, Pearl said, the month of her father's birth. After twenty minutes of a virtually incomprehensible explication of this poem (which Viv didn't know to begin with), Viv tried to butt in and change the topic. Without thinking, she inanely asked her mother how her garden was doing. In response, her mother looked at her as though *she* were going off the deep end and reminded her that it was Christmas and so her garden was not doing much except, ha ha, sleeping. *"One short sleep past"* etcetera. She asked for another drink. She continued talking, telling Viv yet again how much she had loved playing badminton at McGill and how she had once waltzed there with a fellow with red hair, and another time with a Canadian poet, Louis Dudek. As they left the restaurant, she was in good spirits and began trying to sing "I Danced with a Man Who Danced with a Girl Who Danced with the Prince of Wales."

Back at the house, Viv left her mother sitting in the living room with her knitting and a glass of cream sherry while she got the flashlight from her suitcase and went out to the storage shed, which was empty except for the box of Christmas tree parts, three boxes of ornaments neatly labelled, lights and garlands, and gardening tools. There was that stepladder too.

She was less pissed off now. What was doing it? Motherhood? Geographical distance? Age? God, she missed Stella. She closed her eyes and conjured her daughter, two now, the amber eyes, the curly dark brown hair, the open, sweet smile.

When she came back in, Pearl had resumed work on Stella's Christmas present, which was to be a toque and mittens. The hat and one mitten were completed. The toque was huge—too large for any human being. The knitting wobbled in and out like the edge of a nasturtium, hung limp and loose around a huge shallow brim. "I want to add a pompom to the top," said Pearl. Then she showed Viv the first mitten, which was shaped like a high-heeled shoe. She was still working on the second mitten, she said, and she held up her knitting. "See?" This mitten was much larger, about two feet long and over a hundred stitches across. "Thank you, Mum," said Viv. "You've been doing a lot of work. Stella is going to love it." Pearl answered that indeed it was a lot of work, and that she was less than satisfied with the results. When she finished, she would be writing to the people who published the pattern book to complain that their pattern was no good.

As they put up the tree together, Pearl worked with a high seriousness that reminded Viv of the way a five-year-old child might work, and she thought of Wordsworth's poem about the child being Father of the Man, and she didn't welcome the role, if that was what was happening here. Being Mother of Stella was all she was, and all she would be. Amen.

Pearl kept putting the branches in the wrong places. Viv tried to explain the colour coding, and then gave up and rearranged the branches when Pearl was absorbed with opening the other boxes. Viv hadn't finished testing the lights before putting them on the tree when she saw that Pearl had begun wrapping the garlands around it. She wished she was home, home with Frank and Stella, getting their Christmas under way, not her mother's. Out with the old, in with the new.

"I think you should wait on those until we get the other things on," Viv said, but Pearl ignored her. Oh well. Perhaps her mother wouldn't notice there were no lights, and Viv surreptitiously put them back in the box. There were enough garlands for several trees, but Pearl put all of them on. She concentrated very hard and it took a long time. Together they did the decorations next, and there was almost an air of fleeting camaraderie as they hooked the bells and balls onto the branches. It was nearly eleven by the time they were done.

"There," Pearl said with satisfaction, stepping back to admire her handiwork. "Now turn on the lights. Santa can't come, you know, if he doesn't see the lights."

At Easter it was her turn again, and when she arrived, Pearl was again at her kitchen table reading. Proust this time. She was dressed in her favourite gold shoes and red and gold dress, which badly needed cleaning. Her hair was a mess. She looked pale, and thinner. She smelled of urine; the whole house smelled of urine and something burnt. The sink was full of dishes. How long had it been since one of her sisters had been there? Viv propped the back door open to let in some air. Pearl told her to close it. She opened the sliding glass window. Pearl told her to close it. "Whose house do you think this is?" she said. Viv took the giant Easter egg she had brought her out of her shopping bag and set it in front of her mother.

"Shall I assume that's for me?" Pearl said, suddenly pleased as a child.

"Stella sent it. Stella picked it out."

"Who is Stella?"

"What do you mean, who is Stella? Stella is my daughter. Stella."

"I don't know any Stella. Now get out of my way. I am going through there."

Two coffee cups sat on the burners of the stove, with black coffee dregs cooked into the bottom of each. The burners were still on and the cups were hot. The microwave was gone. Most of the dishes were gone. The kitchen floor was appallingly dirty. Viv offered to clean it, but Pearl wouldn't let her.

"I don't need any help from the likes of *you*," she said.

"Okay, okay," said Viv.

"Why is it always you who comes? Where are the others?"

"I don't know."

"I am going to the bathroom. Don't you dare touch a *thing*, or I'll box your ears. Don't think I've forgotten how."

On the kitchen table were various lists Pearl had begun on scraps of paper—including notes on yet another revision of her will. In this version, Viv wouldn't be inheriting books, but her mother's typewriter and her garbage can instead. On another scrap of paper was a list of belongings Pearl was going to sell, clothes this time. The hula outfit from her high school graduation trip to Hawaii. Her father's collapsible top hat. Her wedding dress from 1941. Another was a grocery list. Tuna. Cereal. Milk. Rum. Another was a list of items she had recently sold. The crystal carving knife rests, the toaster oven, a string of pearls, the vacuum cleaner, and all but five of her teacups. Something had to be done. But what?

Back at home, Viv was constantly clenched in her upper arms, her guts, her neck, her back, her jaw. She was impatient, touchy, and found herself handing Stella to Frank constantly.

Stella got on her nerves and she struggled not to snap at her, to remember to breathe, to pass her to Frank when she thought she was losing it. Maybe she was. She couldn't sleep deeply or long. In some weird way her mind seemed puzzled, she told Frank, as though it didn't know something that her body knew. It was like her body was getting a message from somewhere else and not telling her mind about it. "Do you think this is crazy?" she asked Frank. "Or do you think it's possible that my body feels some innate connection to my mother's body, and when my mother's body feels like it's in distress, it reverberates in mine as well?"

"Makes sense to me," said Frank.

"God, Frank. When it comes to my mother, what I need is an epidural for my soul."

"Those would be popular."

Her mother emerged from her bedroom at three and came down the hall clearly displeased to find uninvited guests sitting in her living room. Viv had arranged for the geriatric psychiatrist and his assistant to arrive during Pearl's afternoon nap so that Viv could let them in. Pearl glared at Vivien as though it were her fault. At first Pearl tolerated her visitors' presence because the man was, in spite of his "foreign colour," a doctor, which she noted flat out. But she had little patience with the tests he attempted to administer. He asked her the cost of a loaf of bread. "It costs what it costs," she said. He asked her to remember three things, moved on to a different topic and then a while later asked her to recall the three things, and she did, easily and smugly. But she was quickly fed up with the questions and said she was not interested in playing games with some Indian in a turban. She had an aunt, she said, who had married a fellow "like you" in London, and it had turned out badly. She then rose and invited the doctor and his assistant to leave. The doctor smiled and said they would be going shortly. But first, he said, he had to explain.

"Explain?" she said regally.

"Yes." That if she would not agree to some conditions—taking up her throw rugs, adding rails in the bathroom, accepting help from caregivers and housecleaners on a regular basis—she would have to be removed from her home. The conditions, he said kindly, bore her safety and well-being in mind.

"*I* am not leaving my home," she said stiffly.

"Mrs. Werner, I am sorry to tell you that staying or not staying in your house will not be your choice if you do not do these things I have explained. Now please remember: the mats, the rails, the home care worker to help you. Or else . . ." He lifted his shoulders and opened his palms.

"Or else?" said Pearl grandly. "Ha. Yours is an idle threat. Why don't you go back where you came from? And take your wife with you."

Viv turned away to smile. She walked the doctor and nurse to their car, where the doctor turned to her and said, "Tell me, has your mother always been so . . . obnoxious? Or is this something new?"

"She has always been so obnoxious," Viv said. "Usually she's worse."

"She may not like you much after today," the nurse said apologetically.

Viv laughed. "She didn't like me much before."

Pearl was prepared for the home care worker who showed up at her door the following week. When the young woman knocked and called out her cheery "Hello!" Pearl jabbed a pair of tailor's shears through the chain-lock crack. "You git!" she said. "You git!"

"I have to go back," Viv told Frank.

"What about your sisters?"

"They won't."

"Stella doesn't understand. She just wants her mother. She cries and cries and pushes me away."

"I'm sorry, Frank, I really am. But it's too hard. It's going to be crazy hard enough just on my own."

"Get your sisters to help."

"I can't. They won't. Or they can't."

Viv left the doctor's office the moment Pearl was ushered from the waiting room into the examining room. She closed the door quietly behind her. Her heart leapt with gleeful horror. She cantered down the hall, skipped the elevator and tore down the stairs, suddenly short of breath, her heart pounding as though her mother were after her. Wheezing for air, she threw open the door and escaped the building. Out of the corner of her eye she saw an ambulance pulling up. Feeling panic rising in her, she crouched down behind a half-ton and waited. The doctor would be jollying Pearl along—telling her how he wanted her to go for blood tests and had arranged *special* transportation for one *special* lady.

The doors of the building opened and Viv started to shake as she saw her mother slowly emerging, making her way not like a person subdued or defeated or angry but like a queen being given her due. Two young male ambulance attendants held the doors. She acknowledged the service of her courtiers with a regal yet gracious nod to each. She embarked the ambulance, the attendants closed and secured the doors, and the ambulance drove away.

And that was it. She was gone.

Viv stayed crouched on the ground, her eyes closed, her head tucked under her folded arms. She could hear herself whimper. It was some minutes before she could get her legs under her, stand and locate her car in the lot. More minutes before she could get her legs to take her there, more minutes before she could get the key in the lock, the ignition, the car into reverse and then forward. She drove to her mother's house and she sat in the driveway thinking about cigarettes and alcohol and dope and how she didn't have any of them anymore and wished she had them all. Then she climbed through the kitchen window.

Her mother's absence was as huge and incomprehensible a thing as the absence of God, and as she stood there in her house she felt *bad.* Bad for her collusion in the trickery. Bad for breaking into her mother's house—she wasn't allowed here when her mother wasn't. By entering, she had wittingly violated the laws of the universe.

She turned off the coffee machine and dumped the thick black coffee into the sink. She threw the coffee mugs with the black stuff cooked to the bottom in the garbage. She put her mother's cereal bowl and spoon in the sink. She poured herself a glass of water and drank it. She slid open the kitchen windows. She opened the front door and the back. Welcomed the flow of cool, clean air.

And then she toured her mother's smelly, dirty house. In the living room the knitting bag with the needles sticking out the top sat beside her favourite chair. Her mother would miss that. Viv took four Scotch mints from the Wedgwood bowl on the coffee table beside the chair. Then four more. She put two in her mouth and the others in her pocket. She rattled the two against her teeth with her tongue as she walked down the hall. She turned the thermostat down to seventy. As she went into the bathroom, she crushed the mints with her molars. The sink and tub were scummy. Pearl's Max Factor compact sat by the sink with her can of VO5 hairspray and a tube of red lipstick. Her hairbrush, dirty, full of hair. Her toothbrush, toothpaste. She would want those too. Tiles hung loose above the tub and behind the grubby towels. Around the light switch the silver and green bamboo wallpaper was peeling. Viv pulled a few strips and turned the light off.

Her mother's bed was as nicely made as it had been every day Viv could remember, likely every day of her life, the bedspread smooth, the piping following the edge of the mattress, the gathered skirt falling evenly to the floor, the pillows balanced and even in height, the crease beneath them straight and deep, and no pillow slip or sheet end peeking out anywhere. The heavy floor-length curtains that matched the bedspread—both deep blue and turquoise—drawn open wide to "welcome the day." Every surface tidy, dusty, dirty.

From the doorway of the spare bedroom she glanced at the pictures of Amy, at the unmade bed, at her own book of Cheever stories on the bedside table, her suitcase on the floor, open, her red, orange and yellow underwear falling over the edge, her black jeans in a heap, her socks tossed in a display of carelessness she never practised at home. A little stuffed toy dog of Stella's she had brought for company. The room smelled faintly of herself, and she liked that.

In her mother's study, on her desk, she found two wobbly handwritten drafts of a letter, with a third draft started in the typewriter. The letter, addressed to My Daughters, accused them all of interfering in her affairs. They had put their own mother (this underlined) in such financial straits that she barely had enough to eat. If the whole useless bunch of them didn't straighten up at once (this too underlined) she was going to hire a lawyer to take care of the lot of them at once.

The hospital was badly overcrowded, and Viv couldn't find her mother at first. Was she really here, or had she escaped to return home? An orderly pointed towards what appeared to be a storage room, with its door slightly ajar. Viv made her way past all the people waiting and pushed the door open and went in. There she was. In a wheelchair. Facing a wall of shelves, facing case lots of paper towels and soap, as though she'd been wheeled in straight ahead and then abandoned.

Viv looked at the back of her mother's head above the back of the wheelchair. She almost spoke, but she didn't. She didn't want to see her mother and she didn't want her mother to see her. She would have to refuse to help her. Viv didn't want to struggle with compassion; she wanted to run. Quietly, she put the bag of her mother's things down inside the door and then she turned around and left.

Back at home, Stella leapt into her arms. "I am so glad to see you, Bella Stella," Viv said, and Stella laughed. As she tucked her in that night, Stella took hold of her mother's braid and pulled the elastic off the end. Freed, the braid began to unplait. Viv took hold higher up and shook it like a snake. "See?" she said. "See how it comes all the way undone?"

The night before Pearl died, she summoned her eldest daughter Ruby to the care home, and reluctantly, but with Ativan, Ruby went. They sat together on the edge of the bed looking through Pearl's jewellery. Though very little of it was of much value, the brooches and bracelets and earrings and necklaces all still mattered very much to Pearl, and Ruby said it took forever because she paused as she held each piece. She said barely a word that night, Ruby said, but she handled each and every piece of her jewellery before choosing the necklaces she wanted to wear, placing the others back in the blue leather box and closing its clasp. Then she said with uncharacteristic niceness, "Thank you for bringing me my jewellery." Ruby said it was as though Pearl's displeasure with everything and everybody in the world had evaporated, and there was no tension at all in the air. "I know," Ruby said. "I know, it sounds impossible. But honest to God, we sat together calmly, even companionably." Ruby's words were followed by another long pause, then a half laugh, a mixture of sorrow and derision. "Well, not exactly companionably. This *is* Mum." And the next day, right after lunch, Pearl fell out of her wheelchair and died.

When Viv entered the viewing lounge, the first thing she saw was her mother's sharp nose sticking up like a small mountain peak over the edge of the cardboard cremation casket. Laurel came up beside her from behind, and when she too saw the nose sticking up they started giggling. Ruby and Amy were well behind them, hanging back by the door, silent and reluctant. But finally the four of them were standing in a row, eldest to youngest, beside all that remained of their mother.

The morticians had washed and combed Pearl's hair and it lay short and straight and grey against her skull. The sisters glanced at each other. How particular their mother had been about her appearance, especially her hair. She wouldn't have been caught dead, ha ha, in how it looked now. It had until near the end always been curled and coiffed or about to be curled and coiffed, its finishing touch that chemical halo of VO5. They'd never seen it, never seen her, like this.

Pearl's clothes were as dreadful as her hair. Purple Fortrel trousers and a blue and grey paisley rayon shirt that was far too big and buttoned incorrectly up the front. White cotton sports socks. Her own clothes had been wool, linen, silk. Never would she have chosen such things as she had on. The clothes came from the care home, Ruby whispered. They put on whatever was handy.

Viv was the only one who kissed Pearl, though Laurel, making an odd keening sound, lifted Pearl's shirt and put her hand underneath and touched Pearl's stomach. Ruby, solemn and silent, rebuttoned the shirt Pearl was wearing so that it was right. Amy didn't touch Pearl at all.

Viv couldn't have said later why she decided to kiss her. It certainly wasn't out of love, and she hadn't kissed her for years. Getting close enough to offer a semblance of a hug had repelled her, and it was usually all she could do to make her body go forward to meet hers. Each time it had felt like she was going to slaughter. Maybe she kissed her because if ever in the next million years she wanted to kiss her one last time, it was now or never. She wanted no more regret. Pearl was cold, of course, since her body had been refrigerated, and against Viv's lips her expressionless face, her skull and her skin felt like icy cold concrete covered with rubber. When Viv stepped away, she felt warm air move around her, she felt her own self to be especially soft, and warm, and alive. Immediately she wanted to wipe her mouth again and again. She wanted to wipe death, and her mother, from her mouth, but they wouldn't come off.

Back in the anteroom with her sisters, she felt relief wash over her, as though together they had survived a harrowing ordeal. This was their final visit with their mother; she would go to the crematorium alone, so after this they wouldn't have to see her again for the rest of their lives. The rest of their lives! Hurrah! It was *over*. Viv felt something like joy rise in her. She eyed them all in the big gold-framed mirror. Did they all look different now?

Liberated? "Here we are, Mum," Viv said, waving to their reflection. "Your useless wretches, bidding you adieu."

But it wasn't over. They were out the door and Amy and Laurel were lighting smokes when Ruby opened her purse to get out her car keys and discovered the necklaces that Pearl had been wearing when she died. Ruby apologized: she had forgotten about them. She had had this idea, she explained, that Pearl might like to wear them as she went for her cremation.

"Who cares what Mum might like?" said Viv. "And anyway, she's dead." But no one answered. Why Ruby should care after the way they had been treated all their lives was beyond her, and she said so. But Ruby pulled the necklaces out of her purse in a jumble, sorted them out and hung them off the flat of her open palm. She held them out to her sisters. One was a string of yellow shells, one of brown pods, one of reddish-brown South American seeds, and one of pink, irregular freshwater pearls. Laurel and Amy refused to help. "You go," they said. "We have to finish our smokes."

"Hi, Mum," Viv said as she approached the cardboard casket. "We're back." Then she looked at Ruby.

"You lift her head," said Ruby, "and I'll slip them on."

But that wasn't easy to do. It was hard to lift Pearl's body because she was stiff, and the box she was lying in was narrow. Her head and torso were all of a piece. Viv willed herself to grip and lift. It was like lifting a fallen statue in order to lay a garland round its neck. She shivered as she held her hard mother against her. Her mother's straight grey hair touched Viv's cheek and it was soft, and she remembered being a little girl, maybe two or three, and being carried down the hall to her bath. She had loved the warmth and softness of this body; she had loved to rest her head on her mother's soft, full breasts even while she had feared that mouth, and those hands.

Before she went home to Frank and Stella, Viv drove the fifty minutes south of Vancouver to Beresford and parked near the entrance to the abandoned gravel pit, whose gates now hung open and askew. She walked down the abandoned road about fifty yards and then turned left to push through a bank of blackberries that caught on her coat, and in her scalp, and scratched her hands, until she reached what had been their property. Many of the old trees had fallen over, but in spite of so many new ones it was the same place; soon everything around her seemed familiar again, and she thought she detected, in her, in the woods, a kind of mutual remembering, as though these woods were someone she hadn't seen in a long, long time, and she had forgotten what close and intimate friends they once had been.

The creek too was how she remembered it, the same golden and dark brown, now flowing with a familiar winter swiftness. As she stepped towards the water's edge, the pebbles ground and shifted under her feet. Escaping her mother, she had spent hours here with glass preserving jars, catching minnows. Setting the jar down in the shallow water, sitting back on her haunches, and waiting. There she was, she could see her small self there. Waiting. Waiting.

What a theme that had been in her life. Waiting for this, waiting for that. Waiting for her mother. Waiting for Paul. Waiting to be acted upon, not acting until there was no other choice, until she was teetering between life and death, compelled to choose. For so long feeling powerless to change anything. Until Frank. Until Stella. Hating the past, afraid of the present, blind to the future.

It was like a door had been flung open with her mother's death. Would she cling to the frame? Step back inside where she had been? Or step out into free fall towards who knew what kind of landing after falling falling into the sky? What would her sisters do? Ruby, Laurel, Amy—what would they do? She could predict. And herself? Did she have the guts to step through? Flying or dying. Stella or hell.

She looked across the creek and up to the top of the ravine. The leaves were all off the vine maples; she could see through the trees. There was nothing on the bank but ferns, and above that, empty space. The blue house was gone. All of it was gone. The red chaise longue, the orange and brown carpet in the study, the Danish chairs, the dogs, the horses, the doors, the plate glass windows, her daisy bedspread and curtains—all gone. Nothing but ferns and space and memory.

All those times she had escaped her mother were gone now too. All those times she had dashed like a wild thing out the glass dining room door, slamming it behind her as hard as she could. Heart pounding, she had run towards the ravine with her mother's angry voice chasing after her. She didn't have to look where she ran, and she knew that if she tripped and fell, it would be where the ground was forgiving; it seemed always to be soft where she landed, and she was back up and running in a second. Her feet bumped lightly along the grass of the lawn as though she were about to take flight. She was transformed as she ran into a gazelle, wild and pretty. Not a millstone. Not a nuisance or a wretch. No: she was a greyhound, a cat, a boy.

And now? Now she was Mummy. Belonged heart and soul to her daughter.

She took the pruning shears from her deep coat pockets and began to cut branches of cedar, fir and hemlock. But she'd left her gloves in the car, and her hands were quickly cold and wet, on top of the blackberry scratches, and she paused from time to time to hold her hands between her thighs to warm them, the metal of the clippers digging into her legs.

When she and her sisters had cleared out their mother's room, it was Viv, not the others, who wanted the old photo albums. The oldest dated back to the 1890s, when Gramma Opal was a girl. On the plane, Viv found herself lingering over Pearl's first album, which started in 1917 with her birth. Viv peered closely at the shots of Pearl as a baby in her mother's arms, and in her carriage, then as a little girl, the little girl who had grown up to become her mother. The straight, bobbed black hair and darkly serious expression. Her small face always worried, and unhappy, never smiling. Her fancy little black and white patent leather button boots. Her child's fur coat and ermine muff.

Frank met her at the front door and brought her suitcase and the bags of branches inside while she paid for the cab. She kissed her husband and took off her mitts, toque, parka, and tossed them on the floor beside the bags. Frank said he would make the tea and light the fire while she went upstairs to see Stella. Her body thrilled with anticipation as she climbed the stairs, then warmed with affection as she peeked in the doorway at her sleeping child. She quietly came close and kissed Stella as she slept, letting her lips linger on her child's cheek, and a quiver of love ran through her. Gently she lifted Stella's arm, kissed her forearm, her wrist, the crook of her elbow, the palms of her hands. She sat and just watched her. Adored her. "I love you, Stella Bella," she whispered. Stella, her darling girl. Who had always hugged and tickled, who liked to tease, whose eyes so readily sparkled with good humour. Who forgave all. Who liked to clamber up into her lap as she read to her. Who loved her as deeply and as openly as she loved her. The looks they exchanged, full of trust and knowing.

She lifted her head and looked straight ahead into the dark closet. Had she beamed that same way at her mother? And if she had, how had her mother looked back? Was it always, *always* more in anger than in love? Had she ever, ever just held her close? She stood and sighed in the darkness.

The air downstairs was filled with the smells of the forest. When she had first moved here, she chopped kindling, then laid and lit fires in the small old fireplace Frank had never used. But each time, grey smoke crept out through the walls and into the upstairs; they could smell smoke; their eyes stung. It was not only unpleasant, but potentially dangerous. "Not unlike living with you," Frank had said.

"Well, it's over now," Frank said, standing when she came into the room.

"Yes."

"I think it's safe to say you won't be seeing your mother again any time soon."

"I sure as hell hope not."

He lifted the sleek sterling teapot from the table between them. It had been an engagement present sent from Scotland to her grandparents in 1915. And then it had been a wedding gift to her and Frank from her mother. The teapot was slightly squat, slightly square, with an ebony handle and dainty, strong, silver legs. Just as she had fallen in love with her grandmother's cameos and her wedding veil, Viv had fallen in love with the grace and charm of this teapot the moment she had opened the box in which her mother had so carefully packed it. Next it would be Stella's. Everything would be Stella's. No. Not everything.

"Frank?" she said now. "Do you remember the last time we all visited Mum, and how we pushed her wheelchair along the paths in the care home's garden?"

"It was hard pushing through the gravel."

"Stella was not quite three, and I told her not to pick the flowers, but I told her that she could have the ones that had fallen on the ground. Remember? And then she picked up the dead and dying flowers, all the ones with the bruised petals, the crushed blossoms and broken stems, and she put them all in her grandmother's lap. Remember?"

"I do. That was the last time I saw your mother." A sleek, hot stream of golden brown tea poured cleanly from the teapot's graceful spout. In the fireplace the fire crackled before it began to roar. Money from the sale of her mother's house had fixed the fireplace.

"Are you sorry?" he asked.

"Sorry?" She felt a twinge of anger. "For what?"

"That she's dead?"

Viv paused. Then she put down her mug and took up the poker and savagely poked the fire. "No. No, I'm not sorry she's dead." She thrust and jammed the poker between two logs, levering them apart. "I'm glad. I hated her. Almost my whole life, and I am only beginning to realize how heavy it was carting all that around. You never knew what the hell she was going to do, but whatever it was, it was bad and she would win and you knew you would feel bad bad bad forever. You were always doomed and you had to be on guard. Now the struggle is over.

"She was a grown woman, and she should have known better than to treat me—treat all of us—like that. No matter what had happened to her, and who knows what did or when. I was a child, a baby and then a little child, and I couldn't have known better or worse or anything at all. Imagine me and Stella. Imagine treating a child like that, like she treated me. Maybe she shouldn't have had children and patriarchal society conspired against her, blah blah blah. Maybe she shouldn't have had four children, certainly not four daughters, and she should have been an academic or something instead. But she did what she did. And then she took no responsibility. For her actions. Ever. That's what still drives me wild if I think about it. She never once said she was sorry to any of us. For anything."

Early in the morning, Viv woke up picturing her mother lying cold and hard in her coffin. She thought about how she and her sisters had come out of that body, how each soft new baby had emerged and been held against that breast. What would her legacy be to Stella? Nothing like the one she had received, please God. If she could remain alert, awake to the signs. Please God. She moved away from Frank's warm body and got out of bed.

Dawn was coming. She went over to the window. It was icy on the inside, and it wouldn't open. At least not yet. She went downstairs and into her office.

The old photo albums were on her desk. As she turned pages, passing through time, she thought about her mother. She thought about responsibility and how you had to take it. You had to own up when you screwed up, you had to say you were sorry, maybe over and over and over again, and you had to keep trying. What else could you possibly do and still stand yourself? What else could you possibly do and be a mother? It wasn't about denying or blaming or pretending what you did wasn't so bad. Even if you believed you weren't so bad, when you looked into the faces of people you loved and saw the injury, the pain, the suffering you put there, that you inflicted, no matter how it happened, how could you not acknowledge it, how could you not say you were sorry?

On the wall beside her desk, in an ornate silver frame, hung her grandparents' wedding portrait. Opal's eyes were lifted slightly, marriage ahead of her, promising her, she thought, a happy and prosperous future. How could it be otherwise? And he, Grandpa Mac, he looked hopeful too.

Beside the portrait, the wedding veil hung on a peg. It had been stored in a worn-out Woodward's dress box on a shelf in Pearl's spare room until Laurel had asked to borrow it for her second wedding. When Laurel had tried to wash it, the netting had disintegrated. Pearl had become so angry she said she was going to throw it out, and Viv asked for it. At home in Saskatoon she had gently lifted the veil, a flattened, tattered ball, from the battered box, held it first over a kettle then draped it above an electric frying pan filled with water and turned up on high. All of the wrinkles fell out, revealing vestiges of the veil's former beauty, and even the squashed faux orange blossoms revived somewhat. But the veil as a whole was beyond repair.

In the early morning light, Stella padded into the room and began climbing Viv's leg to get into her lap. "Hi, Mummy," she said.

"Hi, Bella Stella," said Viv. She helped Stella up, wrapped her arms around her and held her close. "I'm glad to see you," she said, and kissed her.

"You're squishing me, Mummy," said Stella, wriggling to get more room, then turning around in her lap like a puppy getting comfortable and settling down. Viv kissed her head, smelled her hair, and together they turned gently back and forth in her office chair. Happy, smiling, Stella stretched out and pointed one little bare foot. It reached and then caught in Opal's wedding veil and then the veil too swung with them, swung prettily back and forth.

Acknowledgements

Dave Carpenter
Joan Crate
Connie Gault
Carolynn Hoy
Robert Kroetsch
Alice Kuipers
Daphne Marlatt
Yann Martel
Patrice Melnick
Ellen Moore
Jacqueline Moore
Elizabeth Philips
Betsy Rosenwald
Steven Ross Smith
Emmett H Robinson Smith
Jane Thorbjornsen Warren
Dianne Warren

Thank you in particular to Janice Zawerbny, editor extraordinaire, who helped beyond measure in bringing the novel to its final form.

Thank you to the Saskatchewan Arts Board and the Alberta Foundation for the Arts for their financial support in the form of grants.

Excerpts from *More In Anger* were published in earlier forms in the *Antigonish Review* and the *Windsor Review.*